Bags of Swank

Thousands marched through O.C.T.U. during their
National Service. Some passed the arduous course,
and were saluted somewhat to their surprise, others
failed, became corporals, and were better paid. David
Walder, a young Conservative M.P., in *Bags of Swank*
has written the most amusing book since the early
Gordons of this difficult apprenticeship period at one
such officer-cadet school.

His three principal characters—Lilburne, a suave
pre-undergraduate; Ransome, non-military but
splendidly militant; and Churchouse, a perfect
poker-backed guardsman of Prussian ancestry—
epitomize England's callow youth scaling this military
height of Abraham. Their triumphs and disasters are
equally glorious.

DAVID WALDER

Bags of Swank

HUTCHINSON OF LONDON

HUTCHINSON & CO. (*Publishers*) LTD
178–202 Great Portland Street, London, W.1

London Melbourne Sydney
Auckland Bombay Toronto
Johannesburg New York

First published 1963

*This book has been set in Spectrum type face. It has
been printed in Great Britain by The Anchor Press,
Ltd., in Tiptree, Essex, on Antique Wove paper.*

'I realize that it is a wasteful and expensive system that trained men have to be put aside to look after conscripts, otherwise conscripts get bored. Regular soldiers must resent an influx of what I can only call unenthusiastic amateurs into the soldier's chosen profession.'

The Author

House of Commons, 1st November 1961

1

'SOME of you will pass and some of you will fail,' said the Colonel. He stood on a raised dais at the end of the long room, his thumbs hooked in his stable belt which alternated bands of maroon and silver. He looked at a mixed collection of shorn eighteen-year-old heads above khaki battledresses adorned with the various permutations and combinations of coloured tape that indicated almost every regiment in the British Army.

He picked up a small cane and jabbed at the lectern in front of him. 'Some chaps,' he said, 'are born to be officers, others can be made into officers, and others,' he jabbed more violently, 'will never make the grade.

'So if you fail here don't worry: it's not a permanent disgrace, you may not become an officer but you may turn out to be something else—a lawyer, doctor, business man, or,' he waved his stick and smiled, 'an artist or a writer.'

'Just as worth while, you know.' He cleared his throat; he obviously didn't believe a word of it.

The Colonel laid the cane down, stared as if fascinated at a shock of bright-orange hair in the front row, and said again, as if reassuring himself, 'Not a permanent disgrace,' and went on to outline the pattern of events for the next three days.

No. 171 War Office Selection Board was a small country house set in the bleakest, dampest part of the Yorkshire moors. Any resemblance it had possessed to a private house had long since been removed. The Army had placarded and signposted every portion of it inside and out from drive to bathroom, as if for the guidance of guests who had lived nomadic lives in tents and caves. Indeed, a Bedouin Arab with a modicum of English could have found everything he desired by reading the innumerable red-and-blue notices. Even persons intended to be officers and gentlemen could have no excuse for mistaking the library for the lavatory.

While there, the Colonel's audience, forty assorted National Service soldiers, each one of whom had been selected by his regiment, would be put through three days of examinations, tests, and interviews designed to prove whether he was or was not capable of holding the Queen's commission 'for the duration of the emergency'.

Popular rumour and the Press have invented many curious stories about W.O.S.B.s and the actual methods of selection they use, from psychiatrists and spies introduced as candidates to judgements founded on school and table manners alone.

The Army, always a good breeding ground for rumour, has magnified these stories to mammoth proportions and now firmly believes them, backed as they are by the sworn testimony of former sufferers. For instance, everyone knew that at 171 the War Office had secretly sent for testing a very young captain with a good M.C. He had been failed as lacking initiative and indeed any other officer-like quality.

The Colonel, stabbing quietly but vigorously with his cane, told his audience that all such rumours were nonsense. The looks of stolid disbelief or tolerant amusement he received in return would have dismayed a politician. He scowled quickly, turned the scowl into a grimace approximating to a smile, and went on with his outline of the programme. Printed sheets setting out the same programme were meanwhile handed round by two unnaturally quiet sergeants.

The aspirants themselves, known hitherto in their own units as 'potential officers' with an obscene adjectival prefix, were to be divided into four groups and would all be numbered and interviewed, would make speeches, do assault courses, and concern themselves with 'group tasks'. Here and there on the programme there seemed to be provision for meals, but otherwise every hour from eight in the morning to seven at night was filled with some form of searching activity. The Colonel was still talking but he had lost the attention of the candidates, who were all more or less covertly looking at the roneoed sheets in front of them. A private in the Intelligence Corps was already making notes in the margin and a trooper in the Life Guards said, as if with his last breath, 'Plimsolls will be worn and there seems to be no time for tea.'

The two silent sergeants were now standing in the wings, as it were, with bundles of cloth squares embroidered with large numerals and with tapes attached. The Colonel surveyed the room, straightened his belt, and pointed at the sergeants with his cane. 'Those are your numbers,' he said, 'we never use names here, and,' he put his hat on, 'good luck.' One of the sergeants yelled, the audience crashed upright, three chairs fell to the ground, the Colonel flicked his cane in acknowledgement and disappeared.

The candidates picked up their programmes and began to collect two cloth squares each from the sergeants.

'Back and front,' said the taller of the two.

'Seven's always lucky, I find,' said the other cheerfully, handing out seventeen.

'Now pay attention,' yelled a voice. A sergeant-major in a glengarry stood in the doorway.

'Tea's now in the anteroom, evening meal 1900, you're free until tomorrow 0800 here, denims plimsolls no head-dress any questions? Right.' The ribbons on the back of his glengarry flicked and he was gone.

The candidates in groups of two or three moved, guided by five notices, towards the anteroom and tea, tying their red, green, blue, or yellow squares round them like deflated life-jackets.

Tea itself was served by two superannuated old men in white coats whose expressions made one feel that they would not have been out of place doing the same service in the Conciergerie during the Reign of Terror. The meal was, however, a great luxury compared with queuing in the N.A.A.F.I., which is what all the candidates had been doing for the last four or five months. They sat down as gently as they could in boots and gaiters and eyed one another warily. Already they had coalesced into regimental groups; one or two who had met previously in the Army, or possibly at school, exchanged a brief nod, but largely they sat and surveyed one another from behind the barrier of their different uniforms.

Conversation proceeded desultorily within regimental groups and as between groups hardly at all. Most of them were looking for the spy they knew would be placed among them and who would report their every word.

Three gunners said they proposed to have a quick look at the assault course before the morning. A Sherwood Forester who looked like a boxer joined them and said that he knew you had to get round in ten minutes or else you were out. A fat young man, wearing rather inappropriately the skull and crossbones of the 17/21st Lancers, said, 'My God!' with deep feeling and took his tea into a corner.

A North Country voice cut across the room. 'My cousin was asked if he hunted. I ask you, in an age of nuclear warfare!'

'It's all a question of boots. I've brought two pairs.'

'Why, for God's sake?'

'Well, they look at them after the assault course and if you've kept them clean they know you've cleared the water-jump and the interview's a piece of cake.'

'Rot, they'll think you avoided it.'

'Well, I'm going to change them in the loo.'

'There's a chap here from the 14/20th with one eye, absolute bastard. Asks you if you drink; if you say "Yes" he says you have to be fitter than the men in the modern Army and if you say "No" he fails you because it would be bad for the mess account.'

'If they're all like the Colonel it shouldn't be hard. Stupider man I've never seen. Typical useless Regular soldier.'

'Really, Daddy said he was the best A.D.C. he ever had.'

'There's a film on in the local flea-pit which is not more than twenty years old. It's about Napoleon.'

'I couldn't bear it, all those useful maxims; dinner and bed, I think.'

'Let's get out of here, anyway, this evening. Is that funny car of yours capable of taking us four to a decent place for a meal?'

'But they'll want you at dinner to see if you eat peas with a knife.'

'Heavens, as if they cared. George Irving got through and he couldn't read.'

'But I thought his mother was somebody's mistress.'

The groups went their various ways: two Highlanders for a walk, the gunners to look at the assault course, three guardsmen to look for an iron for their battledress. Odd unattached souls wandered about, looked at their programmes, and finally decided on baths. The private in the Intelligence Corps was still writing in the margin while four cavalry candidates piled into a white pre-war S.S. and roared away to the nearest hotel. The noise of the exhaust hardly disturbed the fat young man in the 17/21st Lancers as he slept full-length in his chair, the *Tatler* over his face.

In the officers' mess the Colonel had finished his tea and was smoking a cigarette. He looked round at his fellow examiners. 'There was one creature with orange hair, quite distinctly orange,' he said.

'What were the rest like, Colonel?'

'Usual, so young, no M.P.s' sons I gather; anyhow you'll see them all tomorrow and the next day, and the next, to your heart's content.'

'Terrible thought, sir. It looks as if it'll rain and one will have to stand around watching *them* being courageous and longing to break their necks.'

'Tough, you know, Peter, the Army.'

'How's the psychiatric department and their questions? Any new ones?'

'No, sorry, Serial B again this time.'

'Oh yes, "What are your relations with your mother?" One day they'll get a horrible answer.'

'Excuse me, Colonel, but there's a splendid film on at the Ritz about Napoleon.'

'Couldn't bear it,' said the Colonel, 'all those bloody silly remarks about soldiers. Count me out.' He tapped his dog with the toe of his shoe and got up. The Labrador picked up his small cane in its mouth and followed him out of the mess.

2

THE next morning was dull with a distinct promise of rain. The candidates, who were sitting in regimental groups over the remains of a greasy breakfast, looked at one another glumly. The meal had passed largely without incident save that the four cavalrymen, looking pale and edgy, had refused it and demanded black coffee. The fat young man had taken his opportunity and eaten two and a half breakfasts quickly and deftly before one of the old white-coated men had, with a reproachful glance, taken the next away. 'Got a dog, have you?' said the fat young man. There had also been a lot of trouble with someone in the Argylls about the porridge but otherwise their table manners had been perfect. They had not yet found the course spy, though most of them suspected a chap in the Buffs who looked well over twenty and said he had been in the Kenya police. No one believed him.

The sergeant-major in the glengarry appeared.

'Now let's have yer,' he shouted by way of greeting. 'Outside in five minutes denims plimsolls, reds anteroom debate, greens trick cyclist, blues assault course, yellows interviews. Any questions? Right move.'

The Intelligence Corps private opened his mouth. 'But, sir, the programme——'

'Stick it,' said the sergeant-major, not too unkindly, turned about, and was gone.

Outside on what had once been the lawn the candidates lined

up to face a young pink-faced captain, cosy in a British warm, with the green, gold-laced tent cap of the 8th Hussars on his head.

This hat, with its vaguely Mussolini-like appearance, disconcerted the gunners and infantrymen. They were relieved when its wearer addressed them in apparently faultless English.

'My task,' he said, 'is to give you a quick run round the assault course and show you the obstacles. In the midst of interviews and all that stuff you'll come out here in your details and go over the course with a five-minute interval between each man. When you've all finished you'll assemble here and go back to the intellectual side of the business.

'Right, follow me,' and he led the way to the first obstacle, followed by a crocodile of candidates. 'There are twenty-two obstacles, all numbered quite clearly.' This was really no surprise.

'This is the first.' He pointed to two trees about fifty yards apart with a rope strung between them about twenty feet up. 'You climb up this tree, along the rope, and down the other. Quite straightforward.'

So in turn they were shown a plank on ropes suspended over a ten-foot ditch, a sheer six-foot wall, a pole over a pond, some lorry tyres hung on ropes, some massive scaffolding, and finally a sort of gallows on one side of a twelve-foot water-jump. This alone was thought worthy of some explanation. 'Quite simple really,' said their guide. 'A chap will throw you the rope half-way, you jump from this platform, grab the rope, and sail over to the other side.' The fat young man gazed in horror at the rope, the jump, and the water.

'The normal time to get round is five minutes; longer and you will be penalized.'

All now gazed in horror at the obstacles in turn and the distance between them.

As if unaware of the sensation he had caused, the captain said: 'Right, everybody, all clear? That's it, then, back to the anteroom and come out here when your detail is called.'

Eagerly they returned, now and then snatching a quick involuntary glance at the instruments of torture as they passed them. Many had decided that their future now depended upon their performance in the interviews and the written tests.

Even the gunners decided that the obstacles had grown overnight and more than one reflected that perhaps life in the ranks had not been so bad after all.

The blue detail were the first to be called for their preliminary interviews. They sat down in a bleak, brightly polished corridor and one by one were ushered by a sergeant into a room where the Colonel sat flanked by two majors, one bald and fiery in the Warwickshire Regiment, the other dark, scholarly, and spectacled in the Artillery. Before them were virgin-white blotters and piles of notepaper. On their right crouched an Army psychiatrist in a shapeless battledress which appeared to overflow all over his small wooden chair. He was wearing light-yellow socks. The other three officers in the room with him were as properly dressed as if they had been presiding at a court martial. Indeed, this was roughly how they saw themselves.

Outside the door the sergeant whispered hoarsely in each candidate's ear, 'Salute, give your name, rank, regiment, sit down when asked.' He flung open the door and in marched number one.

The Board was treated to a thunderous crash of heels and a muscle-straining sweep of the right hand.

'Sir. Churchouse. Guardsman. 1st Battalion Scots Guards. Sir.'

'Sit down, Churchouse,' said the Colonel.

Churchouse sat down like a pair of compasses folding and removed his cap and placed it on his knees. The Board could now see his face; his fair hair was neat and he looked keen and intelligent. The Board liked the look of him.

'Tell me,' said the Colonel, 'why do you want to be an officer?'

Churchouse's blue eyes looked straight at the Colonel. 'I think I should be reasonable at it, and more use to the Army than in the ranks.'

'Do you think you could lead men into battle?'

'Oh yes, certainly.'

The fiery major looked at his notes. 'You were at Wellington, weren't you?' It was the major's own school.

'Yes, sir.'

'Enjoy yourself?'

'Er—not really.'

The psychiatrist wrote: 'Homosexual?' in his notebook.

'Why not?'

'It didn't seem serious enough.'

'Oh, what games did you play?'

'Rugger and cricket for the school.' The psychiatrist crossed out 'Homosexual'.

'Ah,' said the major, 'not serious enough,' and smiled.

Churchouse stared woodenly at him. His spectacled colleague took over.

'What other interests have you?'

'Music, shooting, and military history, sir.'

'Do you like Beethoven?'

'Very much, but only when he is serious, not in his pom-te-pom moods when he is just a musical Boy Scout.'

The psychiatrist dropped his glasses. The Colonel thought that things were getting out of hand and groped for a straw.

'Military history? What sort of thing?'

'Well, sir, I was brought up on Clausewitz, of course, then I took an interest in Napoleon, but I didn't think much of him.'

The Colonel looked more favourably on Churchouse.

'Then I studied the '14 and '43 campaigns. I was particularly interested in the way in which the pattern of the German advance was identical in both cases whether by infantry or panzers.'

'Er—yes. Any of your relations soldiers?'

'Every one on my father's side.'

The psychiatrist wrote: 'Probably is homosexual', and underlined it.

The Colonel pushed a pencil along the desk. He was about to ask the forbidden question.

'What—er—rank?'

'Three field marshals and five generals, sir.'

'Churchouse? I don't think I recollect . . .'

'Ah, I'm sorry,' said Churchouse, and a wintry smile fluttered across his very still face. 'The initial "S" in my name is for Schmetterling. We were von Kirkhausen until my father was naturalized.'

The Colonel opened his mouth but the fiery major was quicker, he had not won his M.C. in the desert for nothing.

'And your father,' he snapped; 'what does he do?'

'He was a physicist at Cambridge. He is now a director at Harwell.'

'Yes, I see,' said the Colonel—his breath had returned. 'Thank you, Church—er—house, that will be all.'

The Board were treated to another crashing salute. The peaked cap had miraculously returned to cover half the face.

The door closed.

The Colonel looked at his colleagues. 'Why in heaven's name the Scots Guards . . . ?'

'Masochism is common,' ventured the psychiatrist, 'but——' The looks of the Colonel and the two majors stopped him in midsentence.

The Colonel pressed a buzzer.

Number two was the boy with the orange hair. The Board was treated to a quieter salute. 'G. Ransome, sir, the R.A.O.C.'

'Why do you want to be an officer, Ransome?'

'Well, sir, I don't know really, but it's more comfortable.'

The psychiatrist scribbled: 'Sensible.' The Board scowled.

'If you're commissioned, Ransome, you realize we can't guarantee what arm you'll go to.'

Ransome regarded 'arm' as a normal dropped aspirate and said brightly, 'Oh no, sir, there's danger everywhere.'

The Colonel looked puzzled.

The gunner major took another tack. 'You're in the R.A.O.C. now. What's your trade?'

'I'm a clerk, sir.'

'Would you wish to be commissioned in the R.A.O.C.?'

'Oh yes, sir.'

'Why?'

'I like it as much as anything in the Army.'

The fiery major had had quite enough of this. He tried his favourite question. 'You have a revolver, Ransome, what's it for?'

'To shoot myself when I'm wounded.'

The psychiatrist wrote: 'Death-wish in one so young is abnormal.' No one else moved.

'What are you going to do after the Army?'

'Go up to Cambridge and read mathematics.'

'Will you play any games?'

'I doubt if there'll be any time, sir, I want to get as good a degree as possible.'

'Yes, yes, I see, Ransome.' The Colonel bared his teeth in what he fondly thought was a smile. 'That will be all.'

Ransome forgot to salute but wiped a bead of perspiration from his forehead and marched out.

'Christ!' said the gunner, 'they're damned odd, aren't they? But I suppose one has to have chaps who are commissioned to supervise other chaps counting blankets.'

'You know, Mike,' said the Colonel, 'that's a damned stupid question really about the revolver. We all know no one except an expert can hit a barn with a .38 at twenty yards.'

'I know, sir, but it's the psychology of the thing. That's why I rap it out. The chap who says "To kill the enemy", without thinking, has got the right attitude. Chap who says "To protect myself" has got it all wrong.'

The psychiatrist wisely kept silent.

The blue detail continued with its interviews; the Colonel, the two majors, and the psychiatrist passed in review perspiring, nervous candidates, cool, over-confident candidates, and hesitant candidates. The latter the Board thought honest and modest, the psychiatrist shifty and probably addicted to at least one sexual malpractice fatal to the command of four 25-pounders or a troop of tanks.

By the time the son of a Chief Constable had been asked his views on capital punishment, the son of a backwoods Tory peer why he didn't read the *Daily Herald*, and the son of a prominent Left Wing publicist had struggled to suggest methods by which the Regular Army could stimulate recruiting, the Colonel was sick of the whole business. The only two candidates he had liked had been the son of a shopkeeper who said he hadn't a relation in the Army and never had had, but thought he himself would do as well as any; and the son of an engine driver who wanted a commission in the Green Howards because his father had once driven an engine of that name. The Colonel was itching to get to grips with these fellows at his own private interview on the third day unembarrassed by the presence of his pugnacious or his intellectual colleague.

The Colonel regarded himself as a good judge of men when left on his own and was convinced of this each time the psychiatrist disagreed with him. At times he thought of taking the psychiatrist's reports and passing any man who was suspected of being emotionally immature, over-preoccupied with sex, or exhibiting incipient homicidal tendencies. Most of the Colonel's superiors in the Army List had one or more of these vices, he thought. With an effort, he forced his mind away from this intriguing but profitless line of thought and jabbed his buzzer for the last man. It was the fat young man in the 17/21st Lancers whose name was Lilburne.

'Sit down, Lilburne. Are you interested in the Army?'

'Yes, sir. Really, I think, since I collected cigarette cards— uniforms, you know.'

'There's more to it than that. Could you lead men into action?'

'Yes, sir, I think so.'

'You would be expected to play games with the men, what about that?'

Lilburne hesitated. He was about to say 'What sort?' but managed 'That would be all right.'

'What games do you play?'

Lilburne took the plunge. 'Most of them, but rather badly, sir.'

'Does that worry you?' from the fiery major.

Convinced that by this answer he failed, Lilburne said, 'I'm afraid not.'

'Ride?' said the Colonel, remembering the regiment.

'It needs a large horse, sir.'

The Board laughed.

'Any relations in the Army?' said the gunner.

'I don't think so, sir. Oh, I had an uncle who was a war-artist.'

'Really? What does he do now?'

'Nudes, mostly, sir.'

'Does he, by Jove,' said the Colonel, but catching the psychiatrist's eye he stopped.

The Warwicks major, in the best biting tone of the field marshal who had once commanded his regiment, said, 'Got a revolver, what for?'

'I'm not much of a shot and a revolver's not much use, sir, but if there's nothing else it will do to shoot the enemy.'

The Colonel took a deep interest in his blotting pad.

The major reddened, but was not going to give up. 'Do any shooting, Lilburne?'

'Yes, sir.'

'What would you use for partridges on a wet day?'

Lilburne had an insane desire to say 'A knife and fork', suppressed it, and replied solemnly, straight out of a *Field* he had chanced on the evening before:

'Six, sir, perhaps five for old birds.'

The Colonel looked at his colleagues. 'Right, Lilburne, that will be all, thank you.'

Lilburne saluted and left.

'All right, I thought,' said the Colonel.

'Too damned fat,' said the Warwicks major. 'Doubt if he'd get into an armoured car.'

'I must say I thought he was a bit casual,' said the gunner.

The Colonel leant back in his chair. 'Oh, come now, I think you're both a bit hard. He was honest with us. I should think he would get on well with the men. Sense of humour means a lot, y'know.' He looked for help from an unaccustomed quarter. He turned to the psychiatrist. 'What do you think, Doc?'

'Reasonable, normal person, sir, I think. His carelessness is simply over-compensation for an emotional family background.'

'His uncle's nudes, you mean?' The Colonel got up. 'Might shake 'em up in the 17/21st. Old George Barnard's a bit stuffy now he's got command. Perhaps do them a lot of good.' The Colonel left; he had obviously liked Lilburne.

The three other officers began to collect their notes. 'Was six right for partridges, Mike?'

'Oh yes.'

'What's the point?'

'Well, we are told we can ask questions to test the chap's honesty and I did. Nothing more.'

'I thought for a moment it was a forbidden snob-type question.'

'Lord, no, I don't attach much importance to the questions, anyway. Assault course and group tasks are much better to show how a chap will shape up in the field.' He was obviously thinking of Lilburne. 'Don't you think so, Doc?'

The psychiatrist gazed mildly at his questioner. 'Only trouble is, I suppose, that a chimpanzee would get round the assault course in record time. What then?'

'Commission him, of course,' said Michael. 'In some regiments they'd never notice. Provided, of course, he could pass the intelligence test, which I'm damned sure he would. Probably quite good at fitting patterns together.'

So they walked back to the mess to write up their notes for the day.

By the morning of the third day every candidate had answered two question papers designed on the now familiar lines of patterns which had to be matched up, of series which had to be completed, of codes to be decoded, and of groups to be re-sorted. Each hard-breathing candidate had completed the assault course, generally in pouring rain—one had broken his arm on the water-jump. It was a hotly debated question among his competitors whether he had thereby automatically passed or automatically failed.

All had spoken in a debate on the Commonwealth and Defence and everyone had spoken on subjects of their own choice which had ranged from bullfighting to collecting matchbox tops. In groups of ten, each taking turns at command, they had crossed ravines with planks that were too short, climbed a cliff with inadequate ropes, and scaled barbed-wire fences supposedly electrified leading to freedom from a mythical P.O.W. camp. In this, one guardsman had succeeded in getting his nine men over when the wooden platform they had constructed collapsed irretrievably. He turned about, marched fifty yards away, and started to throw sticks at the fence yelling, 'Come on, lads, now's your chance.'

Two examiners stared at him fascinated. One saw a headline, 'Guardsman driven insane by rigours of military sadists'; the other raised his voice, 'What the hell are you doing, Eleven?'

'Sir,' said the young man, standing to attention, 'I thought that if I drew the enemy's fire the others would have a better chance of escaping.' The two examiners looked at each other. They both wrote on their millboards. One put 'Liar', the other 'Excellent brigade material'.

At all the outdoor activities there had been present two or more of these examiners, noting down comments furiously on their millboards. Their presence, perhaps designedly so, was disconcerting. Many a young man wondered whether in order to impress these observers he should, in the group tasks, for instance, show the military virtues of decision and command and thrust himself forward and bully his comrades, or reveal his self-control and obedience to orders by simply submitting dumbly to the dictates of some rather pushing fellow. Most essayed an uneasy compromise. The group tasks were not in fact very well done.

The Colonel wandered round these scenes of physical activity, sitting for a moment on his shooting-stick and looking wise, and now and then speaking to an examiner or looking at an entry on a millboard.

When Ransome fell headlong from a pile of slippery scaffolding to land on his feet he saw the 8th Hussars captain write: 'Willing to take risks.' The Colonel doubted this but passed on. At the water-jump he saw Lilburne on his rope shoot like a bomb over the water to land with a good two yards to spare on the other side. His weight helped him that time thought the Colonel wryly as he watched an examiner write: 'Good.'

A bridge was being constructed across a pond by the yellow detail under the command of the young man in the Intelligence Corps. The supports were too short to rise above the surface of the water and the long runners did not bridge the gaps.

Progress consequently was slow. 'Hurry up, Number Nine,' shouted the Colonel, 'the Japanese are in the bushes!' Number Nine, in the middle of complicated instructions, jerked, lost his balance, and fell in the water.

The Colonel stroked his moustache, avoided all eyes, and walked back to the mess.

There he had a cup of coffee and his first cigarette of the day and prepared himself for the final event, his personal interview with each candidate. At this, alone in his own office, he talked to them, as he would have put it, 'man to man'. He endeavoured to treat them as if they were already officers in his own regiment. Whether his consequent combination of alarming frankness and friendliness ever really bridged the gap between full colonel and private soldier he never knew. Some he thought found it very heavy going and became quite tongue-tied; others, presuming, became too familiar. He changed his questions often, but there were no tricks. He tried to adapt his questions to the man in front of him and so draw him out. As a result, as he told his colleagues later, he often acquired quite surprising information. This time as varied as a certain Derby winner from a cavalryman, a glimpse of Einstein and rays of light that are not straight from Ransome, and a dissertation on the essential need for reform of the present divorce laws from the son of an eminent Q.C. Flippantly as the Colonel later described all this, he took his interviews very seriously and made every effort to judge fairly and without bias.

If the results of his judgements were not always ascertainable one comment at least can be made on his interviewing methods: most candidates on leaving his office were of the opinion that with a little luck they had passed.

3

LANCE-CORPORAL LILBURNE sat rather uncomfortably half in and half out of a 'gin-palace', a converted wireless truck. With his right hand he twiddled with one of the knobs on the wireless set out of sight inside the turret and at the same time tried to disentangle himself from yards of lead caught up with the buckles on the back of his belt.

In front of him along the length of the village street stood five similar trucks, their operators adjusting headsets or fiddling unnecessarily with aerials. Lilburne groped for his map in its perspex case, made a blue cross with his pencil on the dot that represented the village, pushed his earphones up on his head, and adjusted his beret.

Across the street a couple of top-heavy teenage girls ambled out of a record shop and stared at him; Lilburne played with his map-pencil and stared back, and wondered if he should smile or perhaps wink. England has never accepted a conscript army and he knew soldiers were still expected to behave like tough, lustful mercenaries.

'I'll have the blonde,' came the driver's voice muffled by the cab. Lilburne smiled, one of the girls giggled, he shrugged self-consciously and began to flick at the lever of the transmitter. The girls walked on slowly, glancing half provocatively at the occupants of the other trucks. Lilburne wondered what he would have talked to them about if he had had the opportunity. Probably not much, judging from his performance at that dance-hall in Leeds last week.

He felt hot at the memory; he'd just have to make an excuse next time, but when everyone in the hut went it was difficult to refuse so as not to appear stand-offish and snobbish.

He looked at his fingernails; they were filthy again. One of his complaints against the Army was that it seemed quite impossible to keep reasonably clean and this feeling of being dirtier and clumsier than civilians was heightened by wearing a uniform which apart from feeling rough and hairy never seemed to fit quite properly.

Corporal Pickering jumped out of the leading truck and walked swiftly down to Lilburne. 'Did you get that message?' he shouted.

'Reception's not very good——' started Lilburne.

'All right, you weren't listening. Well, you're to go back to the regiment and leave for Upshott tomorrow. O.C.T.U., I suppose.' Lilburne clambered clumsily down the side of the truck; he had been firmly putting the matter out of his mind for the last week or so.

'Good show,' he said on the ground beside Corporal Pickering, and then remembered to look unconcerned in time.

Pickering looked at him. 'Come and have a cup of tea in the café, bags of time to wait here.' They walked across together and ordered two teas and sausage roll each.

Corporal Pickering took his beret off and put it down carefully beside him on an empty seat. He was one of those sad-faced, moustached soldiers that Lilburne automatically liked. The other moustached sort were brisk, cheery, and inefficient, though perhaps even sadder really. He and Pickering were on Christian-name terms, save on parade.

'Well,' said the older man, 'I don't know, Charlie; we were getting on quite nicely and now you're off. I should be a sergeant next year but by then you'll have your feet up in the officers' mess.'

'Actually, I'll be out of the Army.' Lilburne wondered what

long-service regular N.C.O.s really thought about National Service soldiers suddenly promoted above them.

' 'Course, I forgot.' Pickering's moustache seemed to droop a little more into his tea. He brushed away some crumbs of sausage roll. 'I often wonder how they choose you blokes. There's Drayton in 3 Troop, stuck-up bastard—you're all right, of course.' Lilburne failed to disguise his pleasure. Pickering saw this and said 'Yes' in order to mark time.

'Then there's that little chap Yates who failed. What was wrong with him? Wrong sort of school and not enough money?'

Lilburne shrugged helplessly. 'I don't think that matters. . . .'

'Now, nonsense, lad, the Army doesn't change whatever happens elsewhere. I know the sort that gets commissioned in cavalry regiments.'

Pickering, like many of his type, had an inflated idea of the wealth and social position of his own officers. Lilburne tried hard not to look like the son of a duke disclaiming 100,000 acres. He would have liked to cross-question the corporal on the basis of his beliefs and why he was a soldier in such an army. Instead he offered his crushed packet of cigarettes and lit one himself.

'You know, George,' he said, 'I'll miss the chaps up here and it's a nice easy life rolling about the moors. They say they work you like hell at O.C.T.U.'

'Yes, I suppose you will,' said Pickering; he smiled the sad smile of a man with a turned-down moustache, 'for a bit.' He got up to go. 'What I can never understand is if they go through all this stuff at O.C.T.U. how they turn out such bloody wets when they come to a regiment. Do you know, Charlie?'

Lilburne moved to the door. 'Don't know,' he said; what he could never understand was how they kept so clean.

Pickering pushed him through the café door in front of him and gave him a small pat on the back.

Outside the crews of the trucks lounged about smoking cigarettes. Pickering surveyed them.

'Christ, what a lot!' he said out loud. He raised his voice a bit more. 'Leave 'em for a minute and look what happens. Get those cigarettes out and get up on those vehicles. Move!'

He swung round. 'Corporal Lilburne!' Lilburne came to attention and assumed his alert serious expression. 'We'll check the net,' said Pickering.

Bodies climbed about on trucks, wireless operators clamped on headsets and began speaking in unnatural voices into mouthpieces. A few civilians gathered to watch, and wondered why these curious creatures talked to each other by wireless when a good shout would have done the trick for the lot.

Officiously Lilburne peered at one trooper's wireless set and unnecessarily reset the aerial in its socket.

The net completed to his satisfaction, Corporal Pickering waved his arm. Lilburne doubled up to his truck.

'Corporal Lilburne, you can return to base now in your truck. Yates will drive you.' He smiled still, but a little sadly.

'O.K., Corporal.' Lilburne punctiliously observed the niceties of military behaviour and climbed in beside Yates.

'Home, James,' he said cheerfully. They detached themselves from the convoy.

'You're going to O.C.T.U., aren't you?' said Yates. Lilburne nodded.

'My brother was returned to his unit within weeks of passing out for not polishing the soles of his plimsolls,' said Yates reflectively, looking at the road in front.

Private Ransome wished he had not drunk so much brown ale the night before. His hair itched under his helmet and a line of sweat formed under the chinstrap. He shifted his feet in his heavy boots, received a frown from Major Fairbairn, his company commander, and stood still. Ransome knew tomorrow would be Fairbairn's big day, the whole thing under the eyes of all the brass in Western Command, the rehearsal today would have to be perfect.

Ransome surreptitiously wiped sweat out of his eye and tried to remember his instructions. On the appearance of Lieutenant Griffen he was to advance four paces, turn half right and draw . . .

Major Fairbairn looked at his millboard and whispered, 'Now.' Lieutenant Griffen appeared and advanced towards Ransome.

Ransome swallowed quickly and drew his sword.

'I'll cross it, though it blast me. Stay, illusion!' he shouted.

'If thou hast any sound, or use of voice, speak to me. If there be any good thing to be done, that may to thee do ease, and grace to me, speak to me.'

Lieutenant Griffen, his helmet bathed in a grey spotlight, stood motionless and opened his mouth as if to speak. With a slight crackle a record of a cock crowing began to play.

'If thou art privy to thy country's fate,' went on Ransome hoarsely.

'Which happily foreknowing may avoid, O speak! Or if thou hast uphoarded in thy life extorted treasure in the womb of earth, for which, they say, you spirits oft walk in death, speak of it: stay, and speak! Stop it, Marcellus.'

The orderly-room clerk proffered a spear. 'Shall I strike at it with my partisan?' he said.

'Do, if it will not stand,' said Ransome.

' 'Tis here!' shouted a Signals corporal, lunging with another spear.

' 'Tis here!' said Ransome, waving his sword.

Lieutenant Griffen turned majestically in his ethereal spot-light and stalked into the wings.

' 'Tis gone!' said the orderly-room clerk, lowering his spear.

'Now stop there,' said Major Fairbairn.

'We do it wrong, being so majestical,' said the orderly-room clerk and tailed off into a mutter.

Major Fairbairn thrust his hand through his sparse hair and advanced into the centre of the stage. 'You must, must try and look as if you're attacking a ghost. Something you're terrified of.

At present you're stabbing about with those—er—halberds as if you were a lot of drunks—the wrong sort of impression entirely.' He smiled weakly.

Ransome scowled back; he had no stage ambitions, why had he put his name down for this? Hamlet, who was an effeminate sergeant in the Education Corps, was terrible anyhow.

'Now,' went on Fairbairn, 'if we can start Act I again and go all the way through without a hitch I shan't say a word.' A sergeant opened the hall door and saluted. 'Yes, what is it, Sergeant?'

'Private Ransome, sir, wanted for commanding officer's interview immediately.'

'Oh dear.' Fairbairn groped for his cigarette case. He looked at Ransome. 'Yes, you'll have to go, of course, but hurry it up.' He corrected himself. 'I mean if you can.'

Ransome climbed down from the stage and dressed in helmet, doublet, and thigh-boots and carrying a sword accompanied the impassive-faced sergeant out of the hall.

Striding out manfully, Ransome managed to mutter, 'Sergeant, do I change out of this before I see the C.O.?'

The sergeant without slackening pace looked at his watch. 'No time, mate. Anyhow, he's batty about this bleedin' Shakespeare lark too, so why worry? What are you?'

'Horatio, Sergeant.'

'Big part?'

'Not very.'

'Well, they'll have to manage without you. You're going to O.C.T.U. tomorrow.'

'Christ,' said Ransome. He transferred his sword to his left hand and stamped on.

Guardsman Churchouse moved carefully in his best boots round his bed so as not to scratch the gleaming floor and wondered how his second-best cap would fare in his kit-bag. He took an unread copy of the *New Scientist* and an *Economist* from his locker, and, carefully tearing out the pages, filled the cap with them to stop it from crushing. He was quietly pleased with himself. On Memorandum this morning—why orders were so called in the Brigade he had never fathomed—the lieutenant-colonel had been almost affable; had even said 'Good luck' before the R.S.M. had bellowed the orders necessary to get Churchouse out of the office.

He had expected to be called to O.C.T.U. really, but one never knew, his father's nationality had always been a bit of a worry. Being 'Battalion finding public duties' in London didn't allow one much time to think, but now and then at night in bed he had wondered just what they were doing with his papers in Yorkshire or did they go to the War Office?

A rattle of drums drew him to the window, the band was forming up for today's guard-mounting. Only his posting to O.C.T.U. had saved him from being on the Queen's Guard for the first time. His feelings were divided—he realized it was part of his duty, but he had not relished being photographed by loud-mouthed American tourists or giggled at by girls from Whitehall offices. He had heard terrible tales from senior guardsmen of souvenir-hunters who tried to cut buttons off the backs of tunics and of obscene suggestions made by both sexes.

The drum major was barking at the drummer-boys.

Again from stories and from the pamphlets he had read O.C.T.U. was no picnic either. Searching tests of one's military ability plus an inordinate amount of square-bashing, that at least should be reasonably easy after the Guards' Depot. He stepped back from the window nearly to be spiked on the bayonet of a sweating giant in bearskin and scarlet tunic who crashed through the barrack room. 'Some bastards have all the luck,' it gasped over its chinstrap.

Back at the window Churchouse saw the last doubling figure join the three lines of the guard being formed by the C.S.M. A high-pitched yell—in the book for being late, thought Churchouse. A crowd, mostly it seemed of children and old men, was gathering outside the gates of Wellington Barracks.

Churchouse resumed his packing. He had bought a book on a railway-station bookstall about car engines and a paperback on tank recognition, they might help a bit to fill the gap between his infantryman's training and what he would be expected to know at an armoured corps cadet school. He wondered over Major-General Kennedy's *The Business of War* which his father had sent him; should he send it home? He doubted if it would be useful but squeezed it in at the top of his kit-bag, pulling the strings tight over its awkward corners. He smiled to himself at his father's idea of suitable reading for a private soldier. Kennedy's 'I prepared a memorandum for the Prime Minister' contrasted well with his own way of life. A regime of spit and polish and constant drills, broken only by visits to night-clubs by the wealthier conscripts—and there were many in the Brigade—and pub crawls for the rest.

Neither was much to Churchouse's taste. He had once heard three Etonians, hell bent on a wild evening, discussing him—'that dull chap from Wellington, his father was a German or something'. Perhaps he was too serious about what was only eighteen months of his life; still, if he hadn't broken out of barracks without a pass neither had he cleaned latrines for a fortnight, as had one sprig of nobility on returning from one of the shadier night-spots—it was said he had been found out only because the adjutant was there in an upstairs room as well.

Still, three months at Upshott, would they teach him to drive a tank? he wondered.

Outside, the Captain of the Queen's Guard had languidly joined the parade; he brought his sword to the 'order', the Colour lifted jerkily above the mass of bearskins.

Churchouse put his cap and belt on, lugged his kit-bag from the bed, and checked that his railway warrant was in his breast pocket. He stood at the window for a minute; he had got thus far, so why worry? No one had been concerned about his father's nationality at school so why in the Army?—bit different perhaps, as most of his instructors would have fought the Germans.

Anyhow, he wished he knew a bit more about tanks and wireless. Outside, there was an even more prolonged yell, a solitary drum thumped and the pipes begin to wail 'Hielan' Laddie'.

4

MANY towns in Britain have notices on the outskirts, such as 'Mudford welcomes careful road users'. They are tastefully designed in black on white with a coloured reproduction of the borough arms above them; frequently however they are lop-sided or broken, having been struck by passing motorists.

Upshott has none of these. Large notices say, under its heraldic device, UPSHOTT—HOME OF THE BRITISH ARMY. Their effect upon motorists is not known.

The boast is, however, a true one. There are few rivals. Caterham is specialized, and anyhow the Guards' Depot has a competitor for attention in an adjacent but unconnected mental institution. Catterick it is true has a longer lineage, having been a Roman encampment under the name of Cataract, since when there have been few changes save in name and size. It was said during the war to be the largest military camp in Europe, and still spreads over a larger area than Upshott and indeed may still contain a larger number of troops. It is, however, by the criterion of intensity of militarism that Upshott sustains its claim.

Not only is a large part of the town devoted to barracks, schools of instruction, and parade-grounds laid out in a geometrical pattern, but the whole of the residential and shopping areas are also deeply influenced by the fact that since the early nineteenth century, and the era of sham fights watched by Victoria, hardly a

British soldier has completed his service without at some time marching its streets.

The very civilians all have the appearance of ex-soldiers. They are neat and clean and their hair is cut. Few ties are worn that do not possess some regimental significance. Their wives also have the appearance of having followed the drum, and indeed look as if they are about to do so again at any minute. They wear flat shoes and tweeds and often regimental brooches, and are rarely accompanied by any save the smallest children; older ones are, of course, according to sex, either at regimental balls or just in or out of Wellington or Sandhurst.

The commercial life of Upshott has similarly a definite bias towards things military. The shopkeepers themselves tend to be moustached and regimentally tied, and apart from the odd café which is anyway full of soldiers there would seem to be no trade save in haircuts, badges, lanyards and equipment, blanco and boot polish. Even tailors, of whom there are as many as there are barbers, might well drop the 'civil' from their usual advertisement as being civil and military. Their windows are neatly adorned with officers' uniforms with piled leather-covered canes to the flank, now and then a pair of impeccable riding-breeches or a discreet hacking-jacket appearing in the rear rank.

Serving soldiers in uniform, unless scruffily turned out, excite very little comment as a consequence in this genteel Potsdam. The population with their eyes to the front pass them by, their own faces exhibiting that proper look of disciplined lack of curiosity which would have pleased the heart of Frederick the Great himself. Indeed, were his ghost to pass through the town it would be well content. There are at least three shops of military instrument manufacturers prepared to sell flutes.

From the outside, at least, in this military paradise perhaps one jarring note is struck by the cinemas. They cannot show war films all the time, so twice a month or more their hoardings exhibit bosomy lovelies whose clothes appear to be in permanent disarray and heroes whose hair needs cutting dressed in suits made by nameless tailors, leering in a most un-English manner at lascivious stockinged legs which, though pleasing, are essentially ill-disciplined.

The rude and licentious soldier may stare, but inside all is well. The film itself rarely lives up to the lubricious expectations excited by its advertisements and at the close of the performance the rigid backs for the National Anthem would not displease a Grenadier drill-sergeant.

As London Passenger Transport Board points out in its attractive posters, the country frequently penetrates to the town even in modern England. This has not been allowed to happen in Upshott; there are no rural intrusions. The birch-woods and bracken of Hampshire, though desecrated daily by armoured cars, field guns, and trampling feet, have not attempted a counter-attack. The flora and fauna tacitly admit defeat. A sentry-like tulip and a disciplined daffodil maybe, but no more, and although Upshott is perhaps the only town in England where a fox could walk unscathed down the main street they do not avail themselves of the opportunity. Although birds sing and chatter in London, in Upshott they do not, at least not audibly. Dr. Ludwig Koch himself, however or wherever skilfully hidden, would merely record, if his sensitive instruments were not initially ruined, the scream and bark of the sergeant-major and the yelp of the P.T. instructor.

It was into this town, upon which the sun shone as if discreetly to pick out a flashing bayonet or shine upon a polished badge, that some eighty young soldiers were brought by trucks which had picked them up at the railway station.

They sat in the trucks, their kit-bags between their knees, looking at one another half defiantly, half ruefully, taking in one another's military eccentricities of dress, and gaining through the back of the truck swift glimpses of the military life of Upshott. Variously coloured notice-boards proclaimed regimental or corps centres and now and then the wide dusty vistas of parade-grounds were revealed in between the long lines of wooden barracks. A squad of airborne soldiers, their red berets a splash of colour above their camouflaged jumping-jackets, marched by; here and there a provost sergeant stood rigid and house-proud before his shiny guardroom; a platoon of young men in vests and shorts ran over a crossroads and on to a football pitch pursued by a P.T.I. in blue trousers and red-and-white-striped jersey, yapping like a playful terrier.

Their trucks ground their way along Alamein Avenue and Kitchener Way and others similarly named and passed a board labelled 'Ypres Officer Cadet School' and came to rest outside a long row of wooden huts, 'spiders' to the initiated. Wooden huts of similar construction stretched in all directions. Wearily, for they had travelled from their regiments in all parts of Britain that day, the young men got down from the trucks, bumping their kit-bags behind them, and looked around. They stretched and yawned, shook their trousers down over their gaiters, stamping their boots and adjusting their berets on their heads. 'Now pay attention.' An incredibly thin sergeant with the green plume of an Irish regiment nodding in his beret stood before them.

'From now on you are cadets, and in about one hour,' he looked at his watch, 'I shall fit you up with bedding, get your uniforms measured by the tailors, and draw rifles and equipment, discs and tapes and get you back here——' He stopped in mid-sentence, his polished heels crashed on to the ground. 'Partee, partee, shah,' he yelled. The newly created cadets wonderingly but obediently shuffled to attention.

The sergeant's arm flew in front of his face, the hand quivering over his right eye. About two hundred yards away in the mid-distance a figure, just discernible as wearing an officer's peaked cap, sauntered between two rows of huts. This figure, presumably warned by some sixth sense that it was being saluted, flicked its right hand in acknowledgement.

The sergeant stood the cadets at ease and continued where he had broken off: '. . . get you back here as I said for tea—after tea, documentation. In an hour if you move yerselves, otherwise no tea. Now git fell in in threes, move yerselves.'

In some approximation in form and manner to what the sergeant desired, they moved off. In incredibly quick time eighty young men had blankets and sheets. They raised their eyebrows at the latter item, which they correctly assumed was part of their new-found status—rifles, white circular celluloid discs, and pieces of half-inch white tape and great bundles of canvas straps and pouches. All these things were thrust upon them by sweaty quartermaster sergeants whose faces appeared briefly over the half-doors of what seemed to be disused horse-boxes. The visit to the tailor took somewhat longer; there they were measured and issued with clean new battledress which had apparently only one defect. The waistband of the blouse and the legs of the trousers were without doubt at least two inches too tight.

'Like Teddy boys,' said Ransome.

'Last year's style,' said Lilburne, rather too loudly.

'Lovely,' said the tailor, silencing them both with a look. 'You'll thin down to them after a week or two on the square.'

Uninspired by this most curious sartorial recommendation, they picked up their bundles and rejoined the others.

Then in a body they marched back to their huts, threw their blankets and equipment on to their beds, and were told by the sergeant that they could go to tea, but to be back in half an hour for his mysterious 'documentation'.

Tea, or what the Army calls the 'tea meal' and the outside world, especially in the North, 'high tea', turned out to be a surprisingly well-cooked meal eaten in a spotless cookhouse.

Lilburne, Ransome, and Churchouse sat together. Ransome, his ginger eyebrows twitching, had obviously taken the sergeant's exhibition of long-distance saluting to heart. 'What's the point of it all? It won't do them any good in a nuclear war. I bet this place is all bloody bull, trying to be like those madmen at Sandhurst.'

Churchouse fitted a cigarette into a holder, not entirely unconscious of the effect he achieved by so doing. 'You should have been at Caterham for a bit. We polished the studs on the bottoms of our boots there. All for morale, I was told.'

'Madness I call it. Anyway, I don't want to be commissioned in the Guards.'

'Nor would you be.'

'The simple answer,' said Lilburne, 'is that it's all applied psychology. They have to treat officers here with tremendous respect in order to impress upon us the tremendous prize we are being offered. Bait, you know. In fact it's all bogus. When you get to a regiment you'll find subalterns are less than the dirt.'

'If I get to one,' groaned Ransome.

'Oh, nonsense. There are some very curious officers about, as you'll see soon enough.'

They got up, dusted crumbs off their uniforms automatically, waited while Lilburne had a final swig of tea, and joined their fellows who were returning to their assembly point.

'Documentation' proved to be a comprehensive term covering many things.

The cadets sat down on benches in a lecture-room and were handed large forms over two foot square printed on thick crackly paper. They were told by another sergeant, very young this time and of clerical aspect, that these forms would eventually be completed when they were commissioned. Until then they might complete only the lines which indicated name, education, and nationality of both parents.

Arkwright, a gunner, said to his neighbour that he failed to see the point of this as his parents' names and his own would presumably be the same when he passed out as now. If he didn't pass out, on the other hand, this was a waste of paper.

'Bait,' said Lilburne. 'You may have the exquisite pleasure of completing the other columns only if you pass out.'

Despite Arkwright's objection the forms were filled in with

moderate competence. Then they were collected and disappeared under the arm of the spectacled sergeant. He had once had a minor part in an O.U.D.S. production. He knew when to leave the stage.

The cadets waited expectantly and not in vain. The door was thrown open and in walked a sergeant-major, pace-stick and all. He was followed by three satellite sergeants, one of whom was their friend of the green plume.

The sergeant-major surveyed them silently for a few minutes, his eyes scarcely visible under the peak of his cap adorned with the paschal lamb of the Queen's Regiment.

'Gentlemen. My name is Dickens, no relation of Charles, but you'll get to know me all right,' he said hoarsely in a sort of muted shout. 'I am your company sergeant-major while you do your basic training for six weeks. These three sergeants will be your platoon sergeants.

'Officers,' he gave the word a distinctive inflexion indicative of immense respect or contempt, no one could tell, 'will tell you tomorrow all about lectures, exercises, and the like. That's not my concern. All I want from you gentlemen,' one detected the same inflexion, 'is that you'll look like soldiers and future officers and be a credit to me.

'My company, "A" Company, has always been the best and so it will be with you or else I'll know the reason why.' His voice rose higher. 'Christ, gentlemen, you'll sweat and you'll hate me but you'll be a credit to me when you march up the steps.'

The voice dropped again. He had his audience. The cadets stared at him spellbound like birds at a snake. 'Now about appearance.' With a sudden crash he leapt two-footed on to a bench. 'You see my boots?' They were exposed to view. Eighty pairs of eyes looked at their brilliance.

'Yours will be like that in the morning if you have to work on them all night. You can deal with them when the rest of the equipment you were issued with today is up to standard.' A half-smile vanished like the dew in the morning. It was not reciprocated. 'One more thing.' No one actually groaned aloud, but the feeling was there, tangible if unheard. 'Every cadet will wear white tapes on his shoulder-straps tomorrow and a white disc behind his cap-badge.' A long pause. 'The discs are at present three inches in diameter. Tomorrow they will be two inches in diameter and still circular and neat.'

Ransome's face spoke volumes. Churchouse produced a two-inch white circle from his pocket and laid it in front of him.

'Finally, gentlemen, address.' The voice had risen again. 'You call the sergeants "staff", and as for me, well you call me "sir" and I call you "sir" but the difference is, you mean it.' Sergeant-Major Dickens descended from his bench, picked up his pace-stick, and attended by his satellites marched out. Olivier never made a better exit.

The cadets stood up and looked at one another. There was an immediate babble of speech, the general tenor of which was that these sort of tactics might be all right for recruits in the ranks but had no effect on them. 'Who did he think he was fooling?' 'Power complex written all over him.' This conversation over, most reacted practically.

Lilburne departed in search of a N.A.A.F.I. for beer and sandwiches to support his long night's vigil, followed by many others in search of blanco and metal-polish.

One former sergeant in the Education Corps, now a cadet like everyone else, marched purposefully towards the lights in the main administration office building. It was learned later that he had resigned on the spot and asked to be returned to his unit. His wish was apparently granted for he was never seen again. His memory, however, remained evergreen, envy being an excellent preservative.

5

THE next morning eighty young men, polished and gleaming, all wearing white celluloid discs two inches in diameter in their hats, but with their eyes and faces marked as if with the effect of an incredible debauchery, assembled in the lecture-hall. They yawned, rubbed their eyes, and longed for coffee. Those who smoked rubbed their tongues distastefully round their coated teeth.

The night before they had reacted in their own ways to the labours imposed upon them. Churchouse had cleaned his kit in fantastically quick time, producing now and then from his kit-bag buckles, badges, and other equipment worn to an incredible smoothness and consequently easy to clean. The incident of the disc had been no feat of magic, he had been warned and had come prepared.

Ransome, perhaps enraged by an already sleeping Churchouse had at 2 a.m. thrown down all his kit, looked at his blackened and sore fingers, and solemnly proceeded to kick it round the room, cursing quietly and intensely while he did so. He then picked the bits and pieces up, gave them a cursory wipe, and threw himself on his bed in shirt and trousers and was soon asleep.

'Odd chaps,' whispered Lilburne to his three companions.

They nodded agreement and one tapped his forehead significantly. They were senior cadets who had apparently been at school with Lilburne and seeing his name on the list of new entrants had come as they put it 'to give him the gen about this hole'. In fact they sat carefully, for fear of damaging their boots or spoiling the creases in their tight smart trousers, on the edges of adjacent beds, drank Lilburne's beer, and watched him as he polished and rubbed at the great tangle of equipment on his bed. Not by a movement did they attempt to help him; they gossiped about mutual acquaintances now and then, saying, 'Good old Lilly, trust him to have some beer,' tipping it down their throats, or else, 'Splendid to see the great brain of the Classical Sixth labouring away,' and helping themselves to a sandwich.

Arkwright on the next bed, wearing white cotton gloves to handle his brasses, watched them covertly. They had an air of quite unassailable detachment; they were seniors, they were apparently allowed to ride bicycles to lectures, they were superior beings. One said the magic words, 'I shall pass out next week, going to the Greys.' Lilburne cursed them and laboured on, now and then remembering to ask them for useful military information about leave, pubs, and nearby restaurants.

Now, at nine in the morning, all the cadets were back to normal, dressed and clean, their characters masked again, sitting in orderly rows to find out what the powers that be had to offer.

They offered first the cadets' company commander, a Major Hawksworth, a man who bore a marked resemblance to the young Napoleon III. The pale olive complexion, the hooked nose, the greasy heavy moustache were all there, all save the Imperial beard. He wore not a képi and baggy trousers, but the uniform of a regiment in the British Army which since the 1914–18 war had eschewed brass in favour of less conspicuous brown gunmetal. Consequently he appeared to be a study in browns and olive-greens. His tunic was of a drab hue, his shirt and tie had a distinct olive shade, and his badges instead of glittering presented surfaces of dull chocolate to the eye.

The overall effect combined with the dull complexion and the greasy moustache was as of something seen through an aquarium glass darkly.

This illusion was not dispelled by Major Hawksworth's manner While talking he sidled and rolled as if making his way through strong underwater currents. He introduced his four platoon commanders, four fresh-faced captains who looked surprisingly non-amphibious, and went on to tell the cadets what would happen to them in the next four months.

For six weeks they would do basic training and during that period, by means of lectures, films, and demonstrations, would be taught the essentials common to officers in any arm of the service. Elementary strategy and tactics, weapon training, pay, military law, man management, and a hundred and one other things. At the end of this six-week period there would be a three-day scheme, to be followed by seven days' leave. On their return the cadets would begin their technical education in their own arm of the service. Those destined for the Artillery or the Armoured Corps would remain at Ypres. In this part of the course fortnightly examinations, practical and theoretical, as well as many exercises, would be held. A fortnight's camp would complete the course, plus a final written examination.

Each day would be divided up into hourly periods and each day there would be a period of drill and one of P.T. There would also be an early-morning parade 'which will approximate to the shaving parade at Sandhurst'.

'Why?' said an unknown voice.

Major Hawksworth looked for a moment like Napoleon III receiving the news of his defeat at Sedan but went on more firmly, 'Anyone who fails in any way may at any stage be relegated for a month or more or even for the period of the whole course, or,' if anything he looked greener, 'R.T.U.'d, that is, returned to his unit.' He looked into the distance. There must be something more cheerful to end on. 'Ah yes, I nearly forgot, leave is normally granted every other weekend and on Wednesday afternoons, unless of course you are doing extra drill as a punishment.'

He smiled in a weary way. The Emperor had heard that

Bismarck was not such a bad chap after all. 'I hope none of you will have to be R.T.U.'d. There's a lot to do here, gentlemen, don't let it get you down. A sense of humour is a good thing for an officer to possess.'

'And a greasy moustache,' Arkwright whispered audibly.

Hawksworth hunched his shoulders in a Napoleonic gesture and appeared to swim off the platform into the dark shallows at the back of the lecture-room.

The cadets, who had been issued with thick notebooks and pencils and great sheaves of programmes and lecture notes, were by now anxious to begin the processes of military education and some in schoolboyish anticipation were already sharpening their pencils during the smoke break. Education proper was, however, to be delayed for one more introductory talk, this time by the Commandant. As stated on the programme: 'Introduction—Commandant, Colonel H. St. C. D. Mackenzie-Gordon, D.S.O., M.C., M.V.O.'

The picture that the 'Mackenzie-Gordon' had conjured up of some bluff, hearty, tweedy Scots laird was rudely shattered by the Commandant's appearance—to a flurry of salutes from Major Hawksworth and the platoon commanders.

Colonel Mackenzie-Gordon may have come from a line of Highland lairds but the line was either long and had somehow become hopelessly Anglicized, or else was very short indeed.

He was tall—over six feet—thin, and elegant and his recent command of a Lancer regiment had left its impression on his dress. He was the military tailor's idea of a dream officer; his tunic was long and full-skirted, his trousers almost as tight as a pair of jeans, his three rows of medal ribbons looked as if they had been made up that day, his straight fair hair was beautifully cut and one suspected that his nails might be manicured too.

He blew his nose on a coloured silk handkerchief elegantly extracted from his sleeve.

The cadets felt dirty and unkempt as they looked at him. Ransome gazed in open amazement.

45

'Now, gentlemen,' said the Commandant in a light musical voice which seemed to contrast oddly with the bars to the D.S.O. and the M.C. 'You'll have heard all about the dull routine things you'll do here.' Major Hawksworth steadied himself in the shadows against the tide and ducked his head under the surface of his private pond. 'I am going to have a few words with you about the essentials, quite unrelated to each other, y'know, quite unrelated.'

It was surprising what the Commandant thought of as essentials.

'First of all,' he said, 'about the course here. Well, you may find it rather tough and you'll certainly be fully occupied. Still, I have always found the best moral precept when in difficulties is this.' He paused. The cadets were trying to consider what biblical quotation he would consider most apt. 'When rape is inevitable it's much better to lie back and enjoy it,' said their commandant.

'Largely, of course,' he continued, 'you'll run your own lives. In basic training each cadet will command his platoon for a day and later we shall appoint senior under-officers and three juniors. I find the way you chaps deal with each other very significant, but I never pry. If one of you is a four-letter man he'll get treated accordingly. I know chaps get ducked, debagged, pushed out of windows, and all that sort of thing. I want to hear no complaints. I always assume the victim to be a four-letter man.

'Now discipline. Well, of course, the school does not impose it. You may leave if you want to. We have rules for judging officer-like qualities and for making you into officers. You just have to stick to them if you want to succeed. Some of them you may find irksome, but that's just one of the tests.'

The Commandant smiled. 'It's all rather like being at school, you'll find. Most people enjoy it, except, of course, four-letter men.' Ransome felt that he might just as well write the word on his hat here and now, so that he might be recognized. The Commandant took a turn along the width of the room in order to admire his shoes.

'Dress. Most important. Soldiers expect their officers to look smart. You may wear plain clothes off duty. Indeed, I expect you to. One thing, gentlemen,' the voice became more serious, 'hats—you must wear hats. You will all go into Upshott to buy decent soft hats this afternoon.' Major Hawksworth wrote in the shadows on a pad—doubtless his note read: 'Hats'.

The Commandant lit a cigarette. 'Problems. I suppose your only problems will be women and money. I don't guarantee to procure either, but if you are in trouble don't hesitate to come to me.'

One strict nonconformist cadet scowled at the Commandant, who continued to look unabashedly worldly and slightly Edwardian.

'Recreation, plenty of opportunity. I am prepared to grant leave in special cases, y'know—local point-to-point, playing for your county, that sort of thing.' A spectacled serious young man wondered if chess would count and thought not.

'Balanced men,' went on the Colonel, 'that's what I want, chaps who work hard and play hard.'

Lilburne added a hockey-stick and a pair of football boots to his sketch of the Colonel cutting a four-letter man dead in the street.

'Finally, gentlemen, let me say this.' The Commandant stubbed out his cigarette and for a moment looked almost embarrassed. 'You will have the honour of commanding, perhaps in action, the finest soldiers in the world. I trust you will be worthy of it.

'Remember, though, what you are training to be, especially if you think the course is too tough.' The Commandant flicked some imaginary dust off his sleeve. 'Hired killers, that's what all soldiers are to a greater or lesser degree.' The Commandant obviously liked the phrase, he looked at the cadets genially. 'Hired killers.' He contemplated his signet ring. 'Ruthless hired killers.

'Right, Major Hawksworth, carry on, please.'

The Commandant walked out, the cadets standing rigid. Speech Day was over, but no one seemed to have received a prize.

.   .   .   .   .

For the next week the cadets lived in a whirl. They were lectured on what the Army calls man management, they saw demonstrations, they were taught about pay and allowances, and learnt some elementary accountancy. They did P.T., military law was explained to them, and then they were drilled by C.S.M. Dickens. All this seemed at a most tremendous speed so that after their meal in the evening few had any energy left save to clean their equipment and then to lie down on their beds.

Still, as the Commandant would have said if he had thought of it, in time anyone can get used to anything, and after a few days all the cadets began that process recognized by employers, warders, and zoo-keepers everywhere as settling down.

They began to find their way about the school, to notice their fellow cadets and their instructors, and finally to become so accustomed to the tasks imposed upon them that they were at liberty to use their leisure.

Inevitably as each young man became less obsessed with his own curious fate he began to notice the personality of the others. Friendships developed. Lilburne, Churchouse, Ransome, and Arkwright, perhaps only because they inhabited adjacent beds, discovered one another's Christian names and dropped into the normal habit of gregarious animals and moved about together.

They were very different personalities. Lilburne, lazy and humorous with the extreme cynicism possible only in youth, appeared to be older than the rest. Churchouse, already unkindly called 'the Kraut' by some of the others who had learned of his German ancestry, seemed to possess a mania for military efficiency compounded with an extreme romanticism which he endeavoured to conceal under a rather brusque manner. Arkwright was simply one of those Englishmen who make one think that the Phoenicians must have spread farther inland than the ancient historians would have one believe. Ransome was perhaps the oddest fish of all, 'with so many complexes they cancel each other out', said Lilburne. Essentially practical and seemingly indifferent to the Army and yet with a streak of pig-headedness which, if it did not become anti-social, might well stand him in good stead.

Typical was their reaction when they were all four told they were destined for the R.A.C., that is, a mechanized cavalry regiment or one of the regiments of the Royal Tank Regiment.

Lilburne said the uniforms were rather smarter than most and left it at that. Churchouse bought the memoirs of General Guderian. Ransome said he hated horses and swore about expensive mess bills and hoped he could get into the Tank Regiment. Arkwright said hardly anything at all but seemed pleased.

Together like the schoolboys they had just ceased to be they compared notes and impressions on their new masters. Opinions were simple and unanimous and the four platoons of 'A' Company offered no encouragement to the Liberal Party and its oft-professed desire for the alternative vote. Simply they liked or they loathed.

Each platoon liked its own platoon commander and even defended him against the others, but the highest praise went to the fat gunner captain called Tunnicliffe who commanded No. 3 Platoon. Lilburne particularly liked him, he saw the seeds of cynicism more deeply planted in him than in himself. In short, the perfect officer. Unconsciously he adopted some of his mannerisms. The whole company loathed Captain Beaumont who lectured them on elementary tactics and strategy. He seemed too efficient. He was sarcastic without being funny and worse still, perhaps sensing his unpopularity, seemed to compose his thin face into a perpetual sneer. He became 'Bastard-face Beaumont' in no time.

Everyone in 'A' Company became extremely proficient in military law, not because they were particularly interested in the subject but because they liked the instructor. He was a cheerful young man called Mitchell who kept them all amused with a wealth of salacious stories as illustrations, some from his own experience and others from the Kinseyesque activities of the

49

personnel in mixed A.A. batteries in one of which he professed to have had a brother. Everyone laughed and remembered, and Lamont, the son of a Q.C. at the Divorce Bar, made a few private notes for his father's benefit.

Naturally enough, too, the company acquired a butt for most of their jokes. At first there was competition between Parker of No. 1 Platoon and Lloyd of No. 3.

Parker had an unfortunate complexion and consequently soon became known as Pimply Parker, but his main claim to fame was that he talked in his sleep. Each evening he would go to bed about an hour before lights-out, fall asleep, and then proceed to entertain his comrades by gripping his pillow in an amorous embrace and muttering lascivious endearments to it.

Although these were adult, graphic, and detailed, this entertainment because of its essential monotony soon began to pall, even though it was found that with judicious prodding with a stick the recumbent Parker could be encouraged to new peaks of amorous eloquence.

The palm went, however, to Lloyd, as the entertainment provided by this vast, clumsy, fair-haired giant was varied in the extreme. He was a natural-born clown. He first claimed attention by a loud and quite uncontrolled belch during a padre's lecture, but it was his physical clumsiness and apparent ox-like stupidity that gave him the limelight.

Though possessed of enormous physical strength, left and right were to him relative terms and speed quite a foreign motion. He therefore became very quickly C.S.M. Dickens's concept of the third region of the Inferno. Quickly, too, he developed into a lecturer's nightmare; with his pencil grasped in an enormous hand and his forehead puckered he could be relied on to ask the one question that revealed his total lack of comprehension of the whole subject.

Perhaps, though, it was during the daily P.T. that he really became the star turn. Few cadets, especially Lilburne and Ransome, a bond between them, positively liked P.T. but Lloyd did. Before a session in the gym he would, in straining shorts and vest, cavort clumsily about the changing-room like a bullock let out to pasture after a long winter.

Unfortunately, however, faced with some exercise involving co-ordination or neatness or grace he was hopeless. The P.T. instructors who had at first looked hopefully at his physique quickly despaired and soon behaved as if he might inadvertently do them some positive harm.

He fell from a rope, he broke a wooden horse, he crushed a tiny cadet called Clifford as he fell on him, smiling amiably, from the human pyramid.

However, he tried hard and the P.T.I.s had to admit that he bore no one any ill will. Indeed, the very reverse. In a boxing contest one afternoon he caught Churchouse a very heavy but quite accidental blow on the nose. Astounded and contrite, Lloyd dropped his arms to his sides and said 'Sorry'. The P.T.I.s visions of a heavyweight champion faded. The Commandant might have wondered if this particular cadet would really make a hired killer.

Most of the damage done by Lloyd was to himself, though only, as he pointed out rather plaintively, because people tried to make him do things that what he called wiry little chaps could do, but from which he was disbarred by his physique.

Typical was the incident of the wall-bars. As all who have suffered know, one of the exercises beloved of P.T. instructors is one where the victim holds one bar at shoulder height and then proceeds to walk up the others until feet and hands are on the same bar. This is not particularly difficult to the normal person, so that the two P.T.I.s were quite surprised when having ordered this exercise, looking complacently along a long line of straining shoulders and bobbing rumps, they saw one exception to this pattern. Lloyd stood with his arms on the wall-bars looking dumbly and sadly at them like a stalled ox.

The two P.T.I.s advanced upon him, cat-footed and muscles rippling. 'Get a move on, Cadet—up!'

'Can't, Sergeant, tried it, no good, never could, arms too short, legs too long,' said Lloyd cryptically.

'Nonsense, lad, come on. We'll give you a hand.'

An unwilling Lloyd was hoisted bodily until one P.T.I. could force the large feet on to the bar already gripped by the two large freckled hands. The two gymnasts stood back to admire their handiwork.

'Nice, nice,' said Sergeant Barker, 'you can get down easily and do it yourself next time.'

'Tuck yourself in, no need to fight yourself, up with the knees,' said Sergeant O'Hara.

'Christ!' muttered Lloyd. His hands slid off the bar, his legs catapulted him backwards, and he shot between the two sergeants, one of his large feet catching O'Hara in the stomach, to land on his head with a thump that shook the wooden floor.

Watched by an interested audience two sweating P.T.I.s picked up the inert Lloyd and carried him with some difficulty to a nearby bench.

There he sat up, looked at Sergeants Barker and O'Hara, and rubbed the back of his head. 'Told you so, you know,' he said.

Sergeant Barker turned about and yelled: 'Right, all over. Now, gentlemen, something we can all do, with knees bend, arms stretch.'

Sergeant O'Hara, crouching slightly, went outside for a cigarette.

6

AT THE end of a fortnight 'A' Company had been welded mostly by propinquity into a homogeneous unit. It had its own personae, it had its quota of clever young men, it had its clown, it had its likes and dislikes. Also it had enough shared experience telescoped into a short time to give it a life of its own. Indeed, such is the effect of shared experience that by now Ypres had come to represent for its inmates the true reality, with 'A' Company as their special part of it.

Perhaps because of this many of the cadets failed to enjoy the first weekend leave granted at the end of the fortnight. They found themselves talking to parents and brothers and sisters about a way of life that seemed totally foreign to civilian domesticity. Andrew Scovington, their only peer, found explaining his various experiences to his father in his London club as strange, though that father had commanded a yeomanry regiment, as did Martin Peel addressing his adoring aunts over high tea in a semi-detached villa in a London suburb.

Most of them were in fact pleased on the Sunday to get back into uniform, and know that they would be returning to their friends, released from the cloying attentions of relations.

Lilburne found himself reflecting along these lines as he walked up and down Waterloo station, trying not to march in time to the selection of records of waltzes and marches with which that particular station entertains the public. At the moment he regretted having arrived early for his train as he had to withstand the barrage of the curious eyes of private soldiers who looked at him half contemptuously and half enviously. Trying not to look self-conscious, but feeling that he failed, Lilburne tried to hide himself by a bookstall, juggled with his cane, dropped it in trying to light a cigarette, and was finally saved by seeing a familiar figure walking towards him. It seemed to be even less able to control a cane and a grip than he was. It was Ransome. They walked towards each other's white cap-flashes in the manner of Stanley and Livingstone.

'You're early, Charles. What happened, tired of home comforts?'

'Sort of. All I found was my sixteen-year-old sister and her school friend. Loathsome.'

'Oh, I got sick of all the questions. Bloody well sick of them.' Ransome dropped his cane and pushed as if irritated at his beret.

Lilburne looked at him curiously. His face was redder than usual, he perspired noticeably, and his speech had an odd erratic quality.

'I say, George, are you tight?'

'No. No.' Ransome shook his head a trifle too vigorously. 'At least not much, be all right, rather a lot of gin at home. Less now.'

'What about a cup of coffee? We've got plenty of time.'

'Coffee. I wouldn't mind another drink. Why get this train? There's another one just as good later on. Less crowded. Come on, let's have a nice pleasant drink in the gay romantic setting of the station refreshment-room.'

Lilburne looked at Ransome and, impelled as much by curiosity about the new Ransome as any desire for a drink, agreed.

Together they made their way into the smoky crowded bar, moving circumspectly round little knots of private soldiers, for cadets soon learn this habit of diffidence in the presence of the rank and file. 'Incidents' with intoxicated soldiers must not take place; the cadet is without authority but is marked out from the rest by the white tabs and circles liberally sprinkled over his uniform. With his imposed correctness of behaviour and dress and, let us face it, his popularly assumed affectations, he is a natural butt for jokes. His only defence is to be more correct.

Ransome was in fact far from being correct. His beret was now creeping towards the back of his head and he moved purposefully towards the bar, shedding his cane and a canvas grip on the way. Lilburne had already smiled at the barmaid and with what he knew to be a calm voice of authority ordered two gin-and-tonics. She ignored him completely and turned to Ransome.

'Gin. Two doubles and a tonic.' In a minute they were held precariously in his two hands and he was shoving his way towards an empty table.

Lilburne followed him.

'All such a bloody pity,' said Ransome, when they were sitting down. 'There's a simply terrific party going on tonight in Hampstead.'

'Socialist Shadow Cabinet,' said Lilburne, shuddering over his nearly neat gin.

'Socialist, how do you mean? Oh no, no, artists, friends of mine. Probably not your type. Nothing formal. Hardly any debs.'

'I hate debs.'

Ransome ignored him. 'There's one girl called Josephine—Jo—Mason. Quite the most wonderful bosom.' Ransome sketched graphically. 'Trouble is she's a pacifist. Thinks I'm a sort of joke in this uniform.'

'Well, take it off.'

Ransome digested this advice owlishly. 'By God, I will. Next time you must come; let's have another drink.'

'No. It's my turn.'

'Nonsense, absolute nonsense. I shall buy it to drown my sorrows.' Ransome got to his feet and marched to the bar.

Lilburne just had time to look at his watch and note that there was ten minutes to go before another train left for Upshott before Ransome was back. He sat down heavily. The gins seemed even larger and the tonic bottle considerably smaller.

'George, I think we might finish these drinks and catch the next train. I want to get in before ten to do my boots for tomorrow.'

'Oh, to hell with your boots; if we got a taxi we could get to Hampstead in half an hour and still be in the hell-hole by midnight.'

'I have no intention of going to Hampstead tonight, and, anyhow, you are wearing your uniform.'

'What's that got to do with it?'

'You said yourself that this Jo girl doesn't like you in it.'

'But you said take it off.'

'Oh, come on, I am going to get this train whether you do or not.'

With a very bad grace Ransome swallowed his gin and began to collect his grip. Lilburne handed him his cane. Privately he was a little worried about George, he looked as if he might pass out at any minute.

It was with some difficulty that Ransome was persuaded that his beret looked better firmly set on his head and that his belt suited him more if properly secured.

From the bar to the platform was a fairly uneventful journey. Ransome showed a strong desire to waltz to 'Roses from the South' but was restrained under the amused gaze of two ticket-inspectors.

'He'll love square-bashing in the morning,' said one with a wink. Lilburne smiled and then, realizing that for him too the last gin had been one too many, set his face and marched Ransome firmly into an empty compartment and sat him down in the corner. The engine shuddered and clanked suddenly, Ransome burrowed his head in the corner, and the train moved out.

The train journey from Waterloo to Upshott is a short one and Lilburne would have had little enough time for his novel without Ransome. As it was he had one eye on the printed page and one on his half-sleeping companion. He was ready when at Woking Ransome's face suddenly went quite white and he stopped murmuring about the delights of Hampstead.

Lilburne opened the window to let in cold air.

'Thanks,' gasped Ransome, and put his head out and was violently sick into the night. Lilburne moved to one side and lit a cigarette.

The snufflings and garglings ceased and Ransome withdrew a pale face, now liberally streaked with smuts.

'Sorry, Charles. Feel much better now, thank God it wasn't a station.'

'It was, but we didn't stop.'

They both began to laugh.

'Your face is filthy.'

'What, is it? Oh.'

Ransome left for the lavatory and came back some time later still pale but cleaner and neater.

Lilburne himself felt better, and they chatted quietly until they reached Upshott. In the station entrance Ransome began to pat his pockets vigorously.

'It's all right, George, I think we had better have a taxi. I have got the money.'

'No. I've finished my cigarettes.'

'I've only got one left, but you can have it.'

'Sorry, not enough, must have a couple for the morning.'

Lilburne looked round. 'There's a machine over there. O.K. if you have two shillings.'

'Only half a crown.' Ransome searched his pockets. 'No, here we are, let's go.'

As they walked towards the machine, Lilburne, watching Ransome, wondered if even now he was truly recovered. He still seemed to stagger a bit and his speech was none too clear.

'Thank God,' he said as he put his two-shilling piece in the slot and pulled the drawer. Nothing happened. He pulled harder. This time the machine shook but the drawer would not budge an inch.

'It looks as if you've lost your two shillings,' said Lilburne.

'By God, I have not,' said Ransome vehemently. 'I put two shillings in and I am going to get my cigarettes out. Why the hell should they make a profit?' He started to bang the machine with his clenched fist and to pull at the drawer with his free hand.

'You may say that, but how are you going to do it?' Lilburne could have bitten his tongue off as he said it.

'I'll bloody well show you. By initiative and determination and other officer-like qualities.' Ransome's face, still pale after his vomiting, had assumed a greenish tinge in the station's phosphorescent lights. His mouth was set and his fists clenched. Lilburne feared he was still tight.

Ransome began to pound the machine with renewed energy. The noise echoed round the deserted station-yard. Lilburne began to look fearfully for the approach of a policeman. 'Don't be so damned silly, George, you can't open it. We've got to get back. You'll be all right in the morning. You can have my cigarette in the morning.'

Ransome looked him straight in the face. 'Get this straight. I am not drunk. I do not want your one cigarette. All I want are the ten I have paid for. They've got my two shillings.'

'Nobody's got your two shillings. It's a machine. No one will open it for you. If the drawer's jammed it's jammed.'

Ransome had returned to the machine and was squinting through the glass at the packets enticingly piled behind it.

'Wait here, Charles.'

Lilburne watched him as he sprinted towards a taxi-rank some fifty yards away. Lilburne had thankfully picked up his grip when he saw that Ransome, instead of going to one of the waiting taxis, was walking boldly into the lighted wooden hut.

He came out a few minutes later and panted back to Lilburne. 'Just the job, Charles.' He produced a short length of iron piping. He moved towards the machine.

'No you don't, you idiot. We'll finish up being arrested by the M.P.s.' Lilburne tried to grab him but was hampered by his grip. He let go of it as the glass crashed.

'There,' said Ransome. He seized the drawer, at his touch it moved out as if on oiled springs. Ransome extracted a packet of Senior Service and started to tear off the cellophane wrapping.

'All right now, George?' said Lilburne wearily.

'Yes, yes,' said Ransome. He was feverishly lighting a cigarette. 'Except for one thing. You know those bastards have still got a ha'penny change that belongs to me. It comes out of another slot. There isn't one on this machine.'

Lilburne looked. There wasn't. 'All right, they've got your ha'penny, but look at that.' He pointed towards the broken glass and dented front. He found himself adopting Ransome's own phrases, 'You've got even with them now.'

'Yes, I think so,' said Ransome magnanimously. 'I'll just give this bit of piping back and I'll stand you the taxi.' His face was back to its usual colour, his mouth no longer set in line, and as Lilburne watched he walked away quite jauntily to the wooden hut. Lilburne picked up his bag and followed him.

A few minutes later as their taxi passed the now wrecked cigarette-machine Ransome leaned towards Lilburne. 'I still wonder about my change. Why should they, after all?'

'George, give me a cigarette and shut up.'

Ransome obliged and they then sat silently as they were driven back to Ypres.

Lilburne's only consolation was provided by the cadet guard-commander at the gate. On the reasonable assumption that any vehicle after midnight contained an officer he crashed to attention and saluted smartly. Lilburne, relieved at not being stopped and reported late, leaned back in the shadows and returned the salute gravely but nonchalantly.

May 1st, May Day, dawned over Europe. A pale sun shone on meadows and forests, on factories and housing estates. In the East it shone on the steel helmets of the serried ranks that marched through the Red Square: in the West it smiled fitfully on the raincoats of the British Labour movement as its members trudged through Trafalgar Square. To other people in England it was at least the first day of spring, birds sang and men on suburban trains half smiled at typists in gay cotton dresses. England today gave no thought to nuclear fusion or fission, and gave no thought to the two great alliances facing each other across the Iron Curtain. England was at peace and the sword and the shield of N.A.T.O. were not in evidence save perhaps in that great military centre, Upshott. There the sun shone on the bayonets of eighty young soldiers roused half an hour earlier than usual. They stood in awkward groups outside their huts. They knew, but hardly comprehended, that a great decision had been made. Today 'A' Company Y.O.C.S. would go on the square.

The background to this momentous decision was not without significance. Gone, of course, is the day when the British soldier is led into battle by the aristocratic incompetent, gone is the day when courage and a rich indulgent father were enough to make the officer. In a technical age the modern officer must have his complicated trade at his fingertips. The manipulation of the tank, the wireless, and the rocket have no need of spit and polish.

Yet the mystique of the soldier still remains. The cadet must look forward to his passing-out parade, when the band plays 'Auld Lang Syne' and he marches in slow time up the steps, as to the culmination of some almost religious ceremony. For this the acolyte must be prepared. Knowledge of Geiger counters and strontium fall-out are very well in their place but where else can the real spirit of the soldier be inculcated, save on the barrack square?

By regard paid to their deportment and dress, by attention paid to their buckles and boots, 'A' Company had made themselves worthy of initiation into the First Mystery.

So as the sputnik whirled unseen through the stratosphere 'A' Company marched towards the square, C.S.M. Dickens by their side.

Their minds were keyed up to the experience before them, they cast sidelong glances at the other cadet companies also heading for the square, and tried to emulate their practised bearing.

All perhaps save one. As they wheeled at a corner Ransome whispered to his neighbour, 'All right, Charles, about the ha'penny last night, they put it in the packet.'

Lilburne's face did not falter, he stared fixedly to his front. Now borne on the company's ears came the sound as of men in agony, screams and yells, staccato barks, the clank of rifles, and the crash of boots.

And now as they left-wheeled, like Tennyson's level lake, the square itself: its vast sandy expanse stretching out, a slight dust rising in the morning air. Across its length snaked some hundreds of cadets in three ranks, sergeants and sergeant-majors scurrying round them like sheepdogs.

'A' Company was marched to the left of the line, dressed by the right, and stood at ease. They waited.

Down the steps in the centre of the parade-ground marched a figure. It was a large figure, its face was hidden by the peak of a red-banded cap. It wore a tunic, on its left hip high up was strapped an immaculate sword, under its right arm was a pace-stick.

It halted. It threw back its head.

'Parade, stand at ease.' The boots crashed again.

'Stand easy.' The parade relaxed without moving its feet. The dust subsided. The figure spoke. The sound was deafening.

'As there is a new company on parade today I shall introduce myself. I am Regimental Sergeant-Major Muxlow, Grenadier Guards. Contrary to belief, the senior R.S.M. in the British Army is not—repeat not—at Sandhurst.'

A pause while this information was digested and its implication realized.

'I am responsible under the drill adjutant for drill, gentlemen. It is my job to teach you to take a pride in yourselves.'

As the voice continued, pointing the end of each sentence with a scream, Lilburne reflected. He realized he was in the presence of a legendary figure. A man who had drilled half the British Army. Who had in his time sworn and cursed at field marshals-to-be. Who had shouted at royal dukes and who had, it was whispered, given private tuition in saluting to three sovereigns.

The voice went on. The delights of the passing-out parade were sketched. The rest of the curriculum at Y.O.C.S. was dismissed in a sentence as of no import. Then promises were held out that the very cadets would themselves be taught to drill bodies of men. Taught to shout by the Master so that they could command whole battalions and brigades above the sound of massed bands. Lilburne felt that the opportunity was unlikely. The voice, having promised the Kingdom of Heaven, came to a stop.

There was complete silence on the square, broken only by the steady soft crunch of horse's hooves.

'Parade, shun!' yelled R.S.M. Muxlow. Into the cadets' field of vision came a magnificent sight. Mounted on his horse, the drill adjutant. His sword shone, his boots gleamed, his saddlery looked as in the best advertisements for such things. His horse—which had the advantage over its rider of being able to see, for the blue-and-red cap of the Life Guards appeared to blot out all vision—turned and faced the parade. Ransome gazed at this vision. 'Christ,' he said, 'join the modern Army!'

R.S.M. Muxlow turned about with a crash, his right arm jerked up in salute and quivered rigidly.

The tip of the drill adjutant's index finger just touched the peak of his cap.

'Ca' on, Sarn't Major,' he said.

R.S.M. Muxlow yelled, 'Sir!' and carried on.

The drill adjutant's horse with its braided burden walked away to a corner of the square.

R.S.M. Muxlow smartly saluted its disappearing rump and tail, and the back of the drill adjutant. As if controlled by some electronic device sensitive to such compliments the drill adjutant's arm arched slowly but gracefully towards his hat.

The drill adjutant having been removed to a place of safety for the rest of the hour, R.S.M. Muxlow proceeded to carry on. To 'A' Company, the juniors on parade and therefore a target for concern, it was an alarming experience.

Many wonders were revealed in a very short time.

The most important was Muxlow himself. The voice itself had an operatic quality. Arkwright, as he sweated and turned and crashed his heels and bruised his hand as he slapped his rifle, had moments of fancy when he saw Muxlow at La Scala. *Aïda*, he decided, must be the opera, the only difficulty was which role? As physical type-casting has little place in opera he decided that Muxlow could vocally do credit to any. The scream of the 'Eyes right' was well in the soprano range while the deep growl of the oft-repeated comments of ' 'Orrible' was certainly basso profundo.

The effect of the voice was equally impressive. Churchouse, even at Caterham, had never seen company sergeant-majors actually doubling on the parade-ground but they did here when screamed at by Muxlow. Sweat dripped down the face of C.S.M. Dickens as he scurried round his flock.

'Third cadet on the right in the rear rank of your company, C.S.M. Dickens, he's idle.'

'Sir!' yelled Dickens. He was behind Lloyd in a flash. 'For Chrissake, sir, get a grip on yourself!'

Obediently Lloyd straightened his back and lost the step.

'Sergeant—Major—Dickens,' the words were spaced out. 'He's idle twice. Take his name.'

'Sir!' yelled Dickens.

The companies marched on and the voice began to upbraid

someone who seemed to be called S'Major Handsaw. This person, whose name was probably Hanson, leapt about as if galvanized and barked back.

The passing-out troop separated itself grandly from the main body and wheeled towards the steps.

'Senior Under-Officer Houston-Crawford, shout out the time.'

'Nearly ten o'clock——' began an impossibly cultured voice.

'Not that time, you bloody fool, sir,' howled Muxlow.

Senior Under-Officer Houston-Crawford, who next week would be commissioned and entitled to be saluted by R.S.M. Muxlow, went scarlet and yelled 'Sir' as if it were the dirtiest word in the English language.

A few more complicated manœuvres followed without incident save that during a right form Officer-Cadet Vorontsoff, whose grandfather had once paraded the Preobadjentsky Guard Regiment before the Czar of all the Russias, tripped over his own boots and fell flat on his face. His name was being laboriously pencilled down by a sergeant before Muxlow's bellow of anger had really reached its top note.

The companies, again in line, were halted. They looked at R.S.M. Muxlow and he looked at them.

He opened his mouth. Three hundred sets of pectoral muscles braced. Three hundred right hands closed over their rifles.

'No. No. No. No. No. No!' he yelled in a rising crescendo.

Ransome's name was written down because at the first 'No' he expectantly crashed to attention.

'Not good enough. Your fathers—and I drilled them—were much better, gentlemen.' Churchouse and Vorontsoff at least looked doubtful.

Muxlow looked at 'A' Company. 'Sergeant-Major Dickens, your company is thoroughly idle.' The death sentence pronounced by Judge Jeffreys had never sounded worse.

'Even now there's a cadet,' the pace-stick pointed, 'who's naked, stark naked.'

Arkwright involuntarily squinted at his neighbour. MacNeil was clothed. No white body dressed only in boots met his gaze. A sergeant crashed forward and feverishly secured the button on MacNeil's left breast pocket.

'Tomorrow,' resumed Muxlow, 'I want to see everyone trying, really trying.'

The sweat from under his beret ran into Ransome's eyes. It felt like gin.

Muxlow's shoulders appeared for a brief instant to droop. 'Take 'em away,' he shouted.

The companies began to march away, their sergeant-majors howling and yelling.

Company Sergeant-Major Dickens marched beside 'A' Company. At each fourth step he said bitterly to no one in particular, 'When you get the band it'll be murder.' The prospect did not seem to displease him entirely.

Under his arm was a millboard with the names of twenty cadets due to do extra drill on the next Wednesday afternoon.

Dismissed, their rifles in the racks by their beds, their bayonets discarded, 'A' Company some quarter of an hour later clumped, sweaty and dusty, into a wooden hut for their first lecture of the day.

A spectacled captain, neat and clean, stood on the dais. 'I am going to talk to you about the inter-continental ballistic missile. First of all the theory behind it. . . .'

He started to draw a diagram on the board.

Slowly he sketched in lines with coloured chalks.

Ransome looked at the lecturer's hip pocket now revealed as undone. 'Idle and naked,' he said loudly to Lilburne.

The sweaty hands, still shaking from hitting rifle-stocks, began to write down details of the stratosphere.

7

Lilburne wondered distastefully whether to try to clean his fingernails with a blunt penknife or read the letter his father had forwarded again.

He knew what it said, anyway, and there was no single new piece of information he could squeeze out of its terse phraseology. An examination would take place at Oxford for so many history scholarships and exhibitions, including the George Vesty Memorial Exhibition, to those colleges in the Magdalen group on the 13th, 14th, and 15th of the month.

He had applied while still at school but had rather forgotten about it in the hurly-burly of military life; he still wondered who George Vesty had been and what special qualities would be looked for to perpetuate his memory. Obviously he would have to go if it could be managed, but would he get leave? Did the Commandant consider such ambitions as consonant with the behaviour of the gentlemanly hired killer or were leanings towards the university sure marks of the four-letter man?

More important, months had elapsed since he had last read a history book or indeed anything other than paperbacked fiction; what could he remember now of the Holy League or Bismarck's policy towards the German Catholics?

It was heartening to remember what he had been told about Oxford—that there they looked for intelligence rather than knowledge; would they make allowances for his being already in the

Army? Younger dons might, but they had probably translated Greek verse to while away the time between battles, marking the place carefully before they prepared to advance.

Leave, anyhow, was the first essential, he would have to talk to Captain Tunnicliffe about that; surely if you could get leave to play games they would let you off for something as important as this?

Tunnicliffe proved to be obliging and in due course Lilburne, in his very tight best battledress, stood before Major Hawksworth, C.S.M. Dickens breathing at his right shoulder.

'Take four days in all, I suppose,' said Major Hawksworth, looking at the letter.

'Sir,' said Lilburne, very military.

'Good time at the varsity,' said the Major. 'Goin' to row?'

Lilburne repressed a shudder. 'Cricket, I thought, sir.'

'Splendid, splendid,' said the major. 'Good first eleven, Magdalen.'

'Sir, that's only the group,' essayed Lilburne. 'I am trying to get i nto St. Mark's.'

C.S.M. Dickens began to breath harder. Lilburne said 'Sir' again and shut up.

Major Hawksworth smoothed the very smooth hair over his ears and looked sharply at Lilburne. 'Nothing wrong with Magdalen is there?'

'No, sir,' said Lilburne and stared woodenly to his front. He tried to bite his upper lip.

'Ah,' said Major Hawksworth. Just below Lilburne's direct range of vision he pushed at the letter as if it were an erroneous tax demand. He gave the letter an extra push.

'You've seen Captain Tunnicliffe so I suppose it's all right. Probably miss a bit of time on the square, eh, Sergeant-Major?'

Lilburne sensed Dickens's jaw crack into a smile on his right.

Major Hawksworth pushed himself backwards in his chair, another monumental decision taken. 'Yes, very well.'

Lilburne stamped back one pace and began to raise his arm in salute.

'Er—Lilburne, put up a good show.'

Lilburne completed the salute.

Outside in the open air C.S.M. Dickens handed Lilburne the letter with what looked almost like a wink, though he muttered, 'If anybody needs more drill rather than less it's you.' Lilburne took this as dismissal and almost benediction and walked off resisting the temptation to kick at small stones with the highly polished toes of his best boots.

This mood lasted him nearly all the way to Oxford, through two train journeys and a change. He was still in uniform but essentially the relaxed soldier, shoes instead of boots and in the train at least his battledress cuffs undone and his belt discarded.

At St. Mark's a porter directed him to his room, looked curiously at his uniform, and said, 'Hall is at seven-fifteen.' Lilburne walked self-consciously across a quad or two and ascended a flight of elderly wooden stairs and entered a room smelling of unoccupation. He put down his bag and wandered gingerly round the dowdy-looking furniture, looking at the belongings of the undergraduate who normally lived there.

Perhaps unfortunately for Major Hawksworth's view of the undergraduate life there were no oars on the wall, nor, thought Lilburne, would the Commandant have been best pleased by the complete lack of any equipment for a manly sport. The tiny bedroom yielded a dauntingly massive water-jug filled to the brim, and a photograph of a spectacled girl with fluffy hair watching over the bed, but no pairs of well-polished riding-boots nor coiled crops met the eye.

Lilburne, however, was pleased with one thing at least, the undergraduate—his name was painted in white over the black door but it hadn't registered—apparently read history. A fairly large collection of the standard textbooks was scattered over the sofa, one at least could be read before morning. With a little more confidence

Lilburne began to change into civilian clothes for dinner. Changed, he looked out of the window and saw groups of young men walking towards the Hall: smoking his last cigarette he hurried downstairs and walked slowly in their wake.

Seated awkwardly and nervously on a long wooden bench, Lilburne was bored throughout dinner. The meal, served in the semi-darkness of the echoing Hall, was not very exciting and inadequate in quantity by Army standards. For company there were three young men, all three of whom had been at the same school, all three of whom had a depressingly scholarly mien, and all three of whom ignored Lilburne as they discussed the strategy and tactics of the coming examination.

When they had decided that the best plan was to answer a question each from each century, thus demonstrating their overall knowledge, Lilburne lost interest and no longer even tried to look as if he was part of their conversation. In the long gaps between courses he crumbled bread and drank needless glasses of water and stared at an enormous painting of an eighteenth-century judicial figure swathed in ermine and scarlet. The figure, from its superior position high up on the wall, arched its impossibly long nose, consolidated its three chins, and stared disapprovingly back at Lilburne.

He slid away from the table as soon as he could, found a buttery that sold cigarettes, and hurried back to his room. He selected a history of the nineteenth century and began to read feverishly. His fingernails were still dirty, he dropped cigarette ash into a coal bucket—Prince Metternich had been a gay elegant figure at the Congress of Vienna and it appeared one of his Christian names had been Nepomuk. . . .

Lilburne traced 'Nepomuk' with his pen and gave it a princely coronet on his blotting-paper; it was nearly lunch-time. The reading of the night before had given him enough material for three longish essays but no more. He looked along the length of the Hall; youngish schoolboys in need of a haircut still scribbled furiously. Lilburne added a two-headed eagle to the coronet, thinking at the time that this was a rather foolish way of spending what time remained, he could at least check for spelling mistakes. A weary filleted-looking don came in to announce that time was up; two stunted persons in black began to collect the papers.

It was only on the second day that Lilburne ran across Pyke. He had been at school with him and was also at Ypres but senior to Lilburne, indeed on the verge of being commissioned into a Dragoon regiment. Lilburne had never liked him much but the familiarity of schooldays, and perhaps more important the fact that Pyke too suffered at Ypres, made him more than usually pleasant to him.

Pyke stood foursquare in the unfamiliar Oxford quad, his hair too short, his shoes too highly polished, and his hands slightly gnarled by constant slapping against a rifle-butt. Lilburne felt a sudden access of simple pleasure at this sight, and consciously screwed up his eyes and smiled at this fellow sufferer, like himself cut off from the high-voiced schoolboys that surrounded them.

'I hear we get the vivas tomorrow,' said Pyke, 'that is unless our written stuff is absolutely hopeless.'

'I wish to God I knew,' said Lilburne. 'It's just as bad as Ypres and the W.O.S.B., no one really knows. I wish they'd put up a notice in plain English: those interviewed have a chance, those not interviewed none, or whatever the form is.'

'I'm worried about the translation papers,' said Pyke. 'French is all right but my Latin's awful, always was, as you know.'

Lilburne nodded. 'You see that lanky chap over there, told me he's already commissioned in the 60th. Seems funny seeing him scribbling away with these inky little schoolboy wonders. I suppose down here the Army's put in its proper perspective.'

Pyke looked a bit shocked at this heresy, but was probably still thinking about his Latin. Lilburne himself, even while talking, was still trying to retain in his mind some of his quickly acquired knowledge of the night before.

The third day had an air of deceptive ease about it; translation papers and viva-voce examinations. Lists had been posted. All candidates it seemed were to be interviewed, being called away from the examination for this purpose.

Lilburne and Pyke sat opposite each other and worked fairly easily through a French translation paper. Then they picked up the Latin 'unseen', the print neater and seemingly more constricted. Pyke studied it closely, almost held it upside down, and looked across at Lilburne. 'Christ!' he said, and shrugged his shoulders. Looks of disapproval from his neighbours flashed at him from lowered heads.

Lilburne translated steadily.

The Romans were as usual fighting their neighbours and, of course, eventually defeating them and passing them under the yoke.

Mamercus Aemifius was addressing his troops. According to Livy: 'Come, remember the name of Rome and the courage you have inherited from your fathers: turn this fire upon the enemies' city and destroy with its own flames the Fidenae'—whoever they might have been—'which you could not conciliate by your kindness.'

'The blood of ambassadors and colonists, your fellow country-men, and the devastation of your borders call upon you to do this' sounded oddly reminiscent of Hitler, thought Lilburne. Had Roman generals ever delivered these intricate sentences? He doubted it; probably encouraged their men with some dirty joke or more likely with the threat of another flogging. 'At the General's command the whole line advanced.'

Pyke grunted and scratched out and stared over Lilburne's head for inspiration. Lilburne blotted his last sentence. 'Hope you can read my writing,' he whispered, and pushed his completed paper across at Pyke. Pyke stared for a moment and took it. 'Thanks,' he muttered and started to copy it as quickly as he could. Lilburne looked around him. It seemed as if every head on both sides of the long table had turned to look at him. Disapproval and surprise seemed to register behind dozens of pairs of spectacles. It was rather like a Bateman cartoon.

Lilburne met the stares with his best look of bland indifference, trying to raise one eyebrow superciliously. He could never tell if this came off but it felt like it. He waited until Pyke had finished, took back his paper, looked at his watch, and with the maximum inconvenience to his neighbours got up and walked out of the hall to his interview.

Outside he lit a cigarette, looked at the nice blue sky, and walked across the quad to staircase 3. He felt that the Commandant would perversely have approved of his actions, but what about Pyke's in accepting—perhaps he should have refused.

Lilburne knocked on a dark door, heard a grunt, and walked cautiously into a dark little room. At Ypres he had almost got out of the habit of walking into a room on his own unheralded and unguided by shouted orders.

Four dons faced him: one drinking a cup of tea, another smoking a cigarette in a holder. None were dirty, none dishevelled, all were young, spruce, and well tailored. One with sleek yellow hair was wearing—Lilburne could just make it out in the gloom—a Brigade tie.

'Ah, Lilburne, sit down,' said he. 'Just done the Latin unseen? How did you get on?'

Lilburne swallowed and felt himself beginning to blush.

'Well,' said the tea-drinker, 'you want to read history when you come up?'

'Oh yes,' said Lilburne—plainly the Latin paper was not seen as a very great hurdle. Pyke would not therefore be asked awkward questions.

'Any ideas what you want to do when you go down?' Hot water gurgled into the teapot.

'I thought of trying for the Foreign Office,' said Lilburne, again the automatic response. He had no clear ideas about a career at all.

A shadowy figure with one long leg in a green sock extended into the light took over.

'In the essay paper you were faced with three choices: "Boots", "Ghosts", and "Tracing the influence of the nonconformist conscience in Britain between 1840 and 1914". Why did you choose "Ghosts"?'

'Well, sir'—did one calls dons 'sir'?—'I know far too much about boots and I thought the nonconformist conscience had been done to death, anyway.'

'But no one has written a book about it, have they? Made a proper study of it, I mean.' Obviously this chap had set the paper.

Lilburne shook his head dumbly. 'Well, I don't know,' he said, rather lamely he thought. Obviously dons expected one to know. Probably there were scores of dreary learned tomes on this very subject.

'What do you mean, Lilburne, you know far too much about boots?' asked the Brigade tie.

'Well, cleaning them all day.' Lilburne tried to rectify the impression of himself as a bootblack and added, 'And wearing them, of course.'

The green sock stirred so that its owner might look more closely at Lilburne's feet.

'I'm in the Army, you see, at Ypres.'

'Ah,' said the Brigade tie, 'at Ypres.' He considered this rather surprising information judiciously. Had he ever cleaned boots with spit and a warm spoon-handle soaked in polish?

'Not in France, at Upshott,' said Lilburne rather loudly—he had to get this right somehow.

'Ah,' echoed the hitherto silent don in a rather falsetto voice. 'I liked your essay on Metternich but you were very kind to him, would you have been so kind to Schwarzenberg?'

'Oh yes.' Lilburne staked everything on the one fact he had picked up about that presumably significant Chancellor. 'I liked the stiff collar he had made specially to keep his head up at boring parties.'

A falsetto giggle. 'Useful in the foreign service, you think?'

Lilburne smiled his agreement, though deprecatingly.

The green socks shuffled with what was obviously one of Lilburne's other papers. 'Pity about the sheep, you should have developed them much more. One can, I think, see the whole economy of the Middle Ages in the rise and fall of the sheep population. You must look at more manorial rolls.'

Lilburne nodded twice, firstly in agreement and secondly to signify his willingness to embark upon this task immediately if necessary.

'I see,' said the tea-drinker, 'you made some references to music in the eighteenth century. Do you yourself play any instrument?'

'No, I don't,' said Lilburne and added, 'I am afraid.'

'Ah, well,' said the Brigade tie. He seemed to be in charge. 'Thank you, Lilburne.' In the background the other members of the quartet mouthed, 'Thank you.'

Lilburne stood up, nearly saluted out of habit, and instead bowed vaguely at the shadows.

A quarter of an hour later he met Pyke in the quad, fresh from his ordeal. 'God, what a lot! What did they ask you about?'

'Oh, what I was doing in the Army. Seemed rather interested,' said Pyke.

'Looking back, you know,' said Lilburne, 'the only thing that pleases me is that in the essay I got carried away and put quotation marks round one of my own sentences. Probably keep those four egg-heads weeks in the library trying to trace it.'

The return to Ypres the next morning was uneventful. Lilburne and Pyke travelled together discussing alternately hopefully and forlornly what they thought of their chances. Both steered the conversation heavily round the subject of the Latin paper.

At Ypres Lilburne wandered into his barrack room, empty at four-thirty in the afternoon. Lying on his bed an hour later he stirred to the sound of returning feet. He surveyed his companions without raising his head.

'Don't bother to tell us how you held the dons spellbound with your brilliance,' said Ransome by the bed. 'You're on guard to-night.'

'You're not serious?' Lilburne began to move off the bed. 'My kit's all over the place.'

'You can have mine,' said Churchouse, 'except for the boots.'

'My belt would be a better fit, Charles,' from Ransome.

Guard-mounting was at six. For the preceding half-hour Lilburne went through agonies. True, everyone helped, but not one single article of borrowed clothing or equipment fitted properly. At five to six, in a belt too tight and short trousers tucked precariously into the tops of his gaiters, his stomach drawn in and his head held at an unnatural angle, Lilburne marched gingerly on to the square.

An officer and a sergeant-major appeared round the corner of an office block, the cadet guard-commander began to shout. Lilburne in the rear rank for safety slid surreptitiously to attention, repressing the desire to look down to see if any buttons had burst.

The guard consisted of twelve cadets, inspections did not normally take long. The orderly officer, a stranger to Lilburne, glanced cursorily at each cadet and passed on. It was a warm pleasant evening, the cadets, of course, were all smartly turned out, so why bother? The officer flicked his calves with a riding-switch as he walked down the ranks.

The sergeant-major, as in duty bound, took a little longer, a closer stare from under the brassbound peak of the Welsh Guards, but he followed fairly briskly in the wake of his superior. Then he came to Lilburne standing stiff and motionless, his stomach sucked in, sweat pouring down his face. The sergeant-major was touched by this sight of so much honest effort, the lad was too fat, of course, but . . . 'Relax, Cadet,' said the sergeant-major kindly.

Lilburne gasped and endeavoured to show willing, but without daring to move a muscle.

The sergeant-major's face came closer to Lilburne's. 'No need to stand like that. You can stand natural and still be at attention.'

Lilburne tried to remember all Metternich's Christian names and hoped the sergeant-major would go away if he succeeded; Nepomuk certainly and Clemens, was he also Charles? If he didn't concentrate hard he was in danger of laughing out loud.

The brass leek cap-badge came to within an inch of Lilburne's twitching face. 'Relax, I said, and when I said relax that was an order.'

Lilburne shrugged his shoulders a millimetre.

The orderly officer was well down the line swinging his switch now. He shot an impatient glance at the sergeant-major.

Lilburne had moved on to a catalogue of the dates of the main events of the Risorgimento.

'You're trying too hard: stop it at once,' hissed the sergeant-major and hurried off. Lilburne breathed steadily but not too deeply.

The orderly officer having departed, the guard marched off. At the first step Lilburne's trousers flew out of his gaiters, the buckle of his belt gave an ominous crack, he belched loudly, and marched on. Perhaps Oxford might be tolerable after all.

8

ROUTINE, boring routine, coupled with lack of constructive activity, say the critics of the armed forces, is the great enemy of recruiting. Every day in the Press there is somewhere an article or report of the lack of variety and the idleness of the average soldier's life. The two aspects are slightly contradictory, of course. 'Is the Minister aware,' asks the M.P. for Netherford East, 'that the guard-room at Scropeby Barracks has been painted white no less than five times in one week?' 'Recruits read comics all day', runs the headline in one of the dailies. Still the point is made and we in the public are aware that a firm hand is needed somewhere.

The cadets at Ypres were equally certain, but they felt that the firm hand might well be applied somewhere else. They were ready to export their military overseers to any camp or unit that needed reforming and in return receive genial overlords who would allow them to lie on their beds and read comics.

The subject had arisen at breakfast; outside the mess-room rain poured down so the cadets knew that the early-morning drill parade would be cancelled. Consequently they dawdled over breakfast and smoked second cigarettes and cadged second cups of tea from the cook-sergeant.

Churchouse produced a newspaper. 'Listen to this,' he said.

' "Row in the House over Boredom in Barracks. When will the Tories give up National Service which condemns active young men to eighteen months' idleness—a holiday at the public expense?", asked Mr. Frank Lubbery in the Commons today.'

'Come to Muxlow's Holiday Camp,' said Lilburne.

'Wait for it,' went on Churchouse. '"Lt.-Col. Hemingway in a sharp exchange asked Mr. Lubbery whether he realized that soldiers could not be kept marching, drilling, and training every minute of the day. The only real occupation of the soldier was war, and there was none today owing to the present Government's policy."'

'Government cheers, I suppose, and Opposition shouts of "Yah",' said Arkwright.

'How did the worthy colonel get his commission?' asked Ransome. 'Man's an idiot, certainly never been here. What was it, "marching, drilling, and training all day"? If he'd added bulling he would have described this place to a T. Only relief we get'—he jerked his head towards the windows—'is when it rains like hell.'

'I should like to see some of those bastards at Westminster down here, sleeping on their benches half the time and talking rot the rest.'

'Vote for Ransome, the soldier's friend,' from Arkwright.

Lilburne stood up and banged the table. 'It is a great pleasure to have with us tonight Mr. George Ransome whose campaign for justice for the British soldier . . .'

Heads turned. The senior under-officer wondered what those basic-training idiots were doing. Should he exert his authority? A cook-corporal, a jug of tea in one hand and a ladle in the other, stared woodenly.

Lilburne struggled manfully on while Ransome pulled at his trouser-seat.

'We all know handsome George Ransome, we are proud to call him. . . . From pot-boy to politician—a few words.' Lilburne collapsed on his chair, clapping loudly. Arkwright and Churchouse joined in. The clapping became louder when Ransome stood up, scarlet in the face.

Arkwright thought for a moment that Ransome would indeed make a speech. Only for a moment, though. Ransome looked at the heads turned towards him and made one brief vulgar gesture, coupled with a grimace, and strode to the door. There he turned. 'Sods,' he yelled, 'all sods—down with the Establishment.' The door opened beside him and for a brief moment Officer-Cadet Ransome and C.S.M. Dickens stood together.

'Who's the cadet company commander of "A" Company to-day?' he barked.

'Sods,' said Ransome automatically; he stood to a confused attention. 'I am, sir.'

If a rabbit had bitten a stoat the stoat would have worn roughly the same expression as the C.S.M.

'Are you, indeed? Well, Cadet Ransome, you're for extra drill that's certain, but before that get your company down to the drill sheds at the double.' His face came to within an inch of Ransome's. 'Now!' he yelled.

Somehow under Dickens's contemptuous eyes Ransome marshalled "A" Company in the rain and doubled them to the drill sheds. Sweating inside their battledresses and wet outside the company crashed along rhythmically, hating Ransome.

Their destination, the drill sheds, would have delighted Mr. Frank Lubbery, had he ever seen them. They were designed so that if there was rain, what the Army calls 'inclement weather', the cadet should not waste his time or be prevented from practising those complicated evolutions so essential for a mastery of his trade. Within their echoing walls drill could be carried on almost as well as on the barrack square. It was: C.S.M. Dickens saw to that. Indeed the acoustics gave his voice a little extra rasp and bite if that were needed. So goaded, "A" Company excelled itself and soon forgot Ransome, save when as a little extra reward at the end of the drill period they doubled back to their lecture-rooms.

Yet despite the doubling, for which he was but a mere catalyst and certainly not the cause, Ransome was right.

Ypres was change imposed upon change. No sooner had the cadet got used to one routine—and routine is frequently restful and pleasant—when another was imposed upon him.

The six weeks' basic training which had at first sight, when the cadets had arrived at Ypres, seemed to stretch into infinity was now almost finished. Its routine of instruction and lectures, drill parades and P.T. classes was about to be changed. An examination, a three-day scheme, and all would be over. The successful cadets would become senior cadets. No longer new boys, they would move up one company on the parade-ground and they would have proper senior under-officers and junior under-officers chosen from themselves and distinguished by bits of squiggly braid on their cuffs.

It was even whispered that basic training ended the regime of spit and polish, bull was relaxed, and weekend passes were more easily obtainable.

Yet many in "A" Company as well as wondering how they would fare in the examination and the three-day scheme were a little regretful at the thought of moving up a grade.

In 'A' Company they had all got to know one another at least in each platoon, and their characters were, as it were, established. They liked and were used to the 'A' Company routine and in consequence did not want to change it.

So conservative are human beings that the majority of 'A' Company did not want to change C.S.M. Dickens for another unknown. They had grown to regard him with some sort of affection. Major Hawksworth they had grown accustomed to and their respective platoon commanders. Lilburne did not want to lose his indolent gunner officer and Arkwright found himself almost regretting the coming change of one identical barrack room for another. Perhaps this was because these young men were all only a year or less from their schooldays, and schoolboys are notoriously sentimental and conservative by turns. Perhaps this was an aspect of that perpetual human desire to make permanent the essentially transient. 'I wish this could go on for ever,' says the girl on the dance-floor.

Certain it was that these cadets, though none of course said so, felt that responsibilities were approaching and wished to defer them. They were poised between schooldays and manhood and oddly enough, despite the hardships and restrictions, were happy, and secretly they wished to preserve that happiness.

Yet, as is said on a sundial in Oxford, where the same feeling is stretched out for three years under the guise of education, 'The Bird of Time has but a little way to fly—and lo! the Bird is on the Wing'. Responsibilities must be met and progress made and 'A' Company must proceed in its turn to the separate O.C.T.U.s of their chosen arms of the service and to the unknown perils and tests of the 'ten-mile bash', the fortnight camp, and the training in and use of field guns and armoured cars.

One concession to sentimentality was, however, announced, perhaps it was intended merely to mark a change in status. Major Hawksworth had arranged a dinner for the cadets at a local hotel on the last night of the course.

The usual quartet heard this news and reacted in their different ways. Lilburne smiled knowingly and said it demonstrated the cleverness of their instructors. Just before an examination and an exercise which was in effect a test of individual qualities of leadership a prize was announced to be given after the tests. 'Bait,' concluded Charles, looking worldly wise.

'Bait maybe, Charles, but bloody expensive,' said Ransome. 'We all have to fork out thirty bob.'

'Some of it's pooled, though, for drinks,' Arkwright observed.

'Yes, I know, some of which will be drunk by C.S.M. Dickens and his crew of torturers.'

'Yes, George, but don't worry, you'll be able to have your fill. I think what you really object to is having to pay for food.'

'Really, Peter, you'd think I was becoming a drunk.'

Lilburne raised his eyebrows. 'Becoming?' He was about to

mention the cigarette-machine incident but decided against it; since that night it had been a close secret between George an himself. Better leave it so. He turned to Churchouse. 'What about you, Nick, any views about the jolly outing organized for us?'

Churchouse looked at them very solemnly. 'I was thinking,' he said, 'that as we go on leave, to return Armoured Corps cadets, it will be the last occasion on which I shall wear my badge.' He indicated the star of the Scots Guards gleaming in his peaked cap. 'It seems a pity.'

Arkwright stared at him and then said roughly, 'You can keep it at home and give it to your grandchildren.'

Two pale-blue eyes stared back at him. 'I shall do that,' said Churchouse, quite simply, and turned and walked away.

Was his back perhaps a little straighter than usual?

Arkwright, Ransome, and Lilburne looked at one another in amazement. 'Charles, he took what I said seriously and his answer —he meant that, you know.'

Lilburne shrugged his shoulders. 'Oh yes, I know, very un-English.'

'Odd lot, the Germans,' said Ransome and embarked on some rambling story about a relation of his who had been thrown out of the Bayreuth Festival in 1938. On the whole it sounded as if he had deserved it.

'Charles,' said Churchouse later, 'what are you doing for your week's leave?'

'Well, Nick, I suppose I shall have to see my parents but nothing very much, I should imagine.' Lilburne automatically hesitated on his right heel to put himself in step.

They had just finished their examination papers for their basic training and were now going to draw maps and compasses for the end-of-course exercise.

'I wondered if you would like to spend two or three days with me? We live in Bucks and I am sure my parents would like to see you.'

Automatically Lilburne, who was a sociable soul, agreed.

'Then we'll sort out dates after the scheme and I'll give you a ring in London.'

'Splendid, I'd love to come—if we both survive the coming three days, that is.'

'Of course. If we both survive,' smiled Churchouse.

Lilburne looked at him and smiled back. In the last few weeks he and Nick had become closer. He liked him. One evening in the N.A.A.F.I., after a preliminary chat about music, a mutual interest, Churchouse had suddenly blurted out what Charles had already half guessed. That Churchouse, the naturalized half-German, was desperately anxious to succeed as a soldier, as a British soldier. Somehow as if the commissioning of Churchouse junior in a cavalry regiment would set the seal of respectability and acceptance on the naturalization of Churchouse senior.

As to the invitation, Lilburne had no regrets about accepting that. The alternative would have been five days spent in London in a half-empty house with the two duty lunches, one with his mother who would criticize his father, the other with his father who would criticize his mother. If these two dates could be arranged for the Monday and the Friday, leaving a gap in between, the gap could well be spent *chez* Churchouse.

Nick produced a small diary and thumbed through the pages. He began to make notes with a pencil. Everything, it seemed, went down in this small diary. Lilburne wondered if it had entries such as 'Get up', 'Shave', and 'Go to bed'. It was a platoon joke that if you took away Churchouse's diary he would probably cease to function.

'I see they've shifted the extra drill we've earned to Tuesday, then we've got Wednesday, Thursday, and Friday for the scheme.'

'We all have to have our hair cut tomorrow morning,' interrupted Charles.

'Yes, I have that in the margin,' said Nick, unblinking, 'so if you could come to us on Wednesday, say, next week and stay till Friday.'

'Right,' said Charles, 'I'll try and ring my parents tomorrow afternoon. I suppose there'll be a damn' great queue for that ridiculous single machine in the guardroom. I shan't be popular, as it means two calls.'

'Two calls,' said Nick. 'I don't see why.'

'Difficult, really.' Charles shrugged his shoulders. 'They're separated. I suppose both will have to come to the passing-out parade if and when, but unless I arrange to have them at opposite ends of the enclosure they'll probably fight during the General Salute.'

'Parents are asked, Charles, are they?'

'Oh yes, two per man.'

'I wonder if we really will pass out in July?'

'Good God, you should worry, you at least are certain to——'

Nick shook his head. 'I wonder sometimes whether we shouldn't talk about it. Things always go wrong, you know, if you do. The gods,' he pointed upwards, 'they watch us and trip up our little schemes.'

'And kill us for their sport, you mean? Excessive hubris and all that.' Charles twitched an imaginary pace-stick under his arm and produced a passable imitation of Muxlow's voice. 'Any cadet suffering from excessive hubris or delusions of grandeur will report to the Olympian drill square at 0900 hours for drill under C.S.M. Mars. Captain Zeus will command the parade. Thunderbolts will be drawn from the Q.M. stores at 0830.'

Nick pushed his cap farther over his face and growled, 'Music for the parade will be provided by a choir of sirens under Bandmaster, First Class, Orpheus.'

When they reached the Q.M. stores they were still smiling, but managed to ask for compasses and maps with straight faces.

The R.Q.M.S. looked at them sourly over his wooden counter. 'You two cadets are late—why?'

Charles stood to attention. 'Well, sir, we've both been suffering from hubris, sir, and we had to be examined.'

'Oh, well.' The compasses and maps were slapped on the counter and signed for.

The door was only half closed when the R.Q.M.S. said to his assistant: 'Christ, Harry, you wouldn't think it at their age, would you? I knew a chap in the Black Watch in India who had it bad. Caught it in the bazaar. . . .'

Unwillingly, Nick closed the door.

Despite the Churchouse diary scheme and unaccustomed hurry on his own part Charles found gaining an opportunity to telephone his parents on Tuesday an undertaking fraught with difficulty.

He had thought an opportunity might occur after his haircut, but he was last in the queue and had to watch glumly while Franz Josef deftly clipped at heads with what seemed positively finicky detail.

Franz Josef was the Commandant's idea. Certain it was that he was of some undefined Middle European nationality, but exactly how he had arrived at Ypres was a mystery. The best theory was that Colonel Mackenzie-Gordon had seduced him away from Trumper's or, as some would have it, some hotel on the Vienna Ring-strasse. With his fringe of beautiful white curls and his courtly manner the latter seemed more likely. He looked more as if he had cut the hair of the Crown Prince Rudolph than that of the youthful Sitwell brothers.

The name Franz Josef had of course been coined by the second, or Viennese, school of thought among the cadets. Everyone agreed that the Commandant's idea had been a good one. The rule 'the hair of the head will be short' was observed, but hair was cut well and not cropped roughly. Mackenzie-Gordon's theory that the young men entrusted to his care should look like gentlemen, even if short-haired gentlemen, was put into practice.

Today, however, Charles didn't care if Franz Josef dropped the haircutting standards of a lifetime and assumed those of the

Prussian Guard or an Australian sheep-shearing competition so long as he would hurry up.

He didn't. Charles's hair was cut meticulously but it appeared maddeningly slowly so that he had time only to snatch a quick lunch in order to collect his rifle and bayonet in time for extra drill at two o'clock.

Four times during these rushings to and fro he had passed the guardroom telephone, enticingly unoccupied, but with no time to use it. So, with the twenty other cadets who had lost their names during the week, Charles marched to the square in the blazing afternoon sun in no very pleasant temper.

Extra drill did not help. It was designed as a punishment and was controlled by a sergeant-major and a sergeant who also thereby lost their afternoon off. The combination did not make them more than usually tolerant of the eccentricities of the 'young gentlemen'.

This afternoon everything was done in double-quick time. Marching, for instance, at one hundred and eighty paces to the minute at the behest of a granite-faced sergeant-major in the Royal Scots whose voice took on an almost religious note as he screamed and shouted. Indeed, the effect of a pronounced Scots accent to give importance and a kind of honesty to the simplest statement became apparent. No cadet minded by now being called ''Orrible' or being told that his drill was terrible. 'Horrrrible' and 'Turrrible' and 'Dusgrraceful', though, seemed much more serious. Even the constant 'Noo, noo, noo, as ye wurr' seemed to contain Knoxian moral undertones.

At last, his ingenuity strained by ordering the cadets to carry out a right form difficult enough ordinarily and almost impossible in double-quick time, Sergeant-Major Macfarlane called them to a ragged halt. Enforced speed had brought them to a sorry state of confusion. Their faces ran with sweat and their gaiters were awry. Serge and sweat had chafed their armpits.

'Noo,' said Macfarlane, 'it's half time, so a few questions to test your mental alertness.' The cadets stood at ease, not caring whether they were mentally alert or not. At least they would not be moving for ten minutes. Butcher Cumberland and Dr. Johnson's views on the Scots were as nothing to theirs.

'Noo,' said Macfarlane, 'a simple one to start with. What's the name of the senior R.A.C. instructorr here? Yew.' He pointed at MacNeil.

'Dawson, sir.'

'What! Never let me hear you say that again, Cadet. Major Dawson, the King's Dragoon Guards, is the right answer. Double round the square with your rifle above your head. "Dawson" indeed, verra, verra rude.'

Nineteen sweating figures looked at Macfarlane in horror. MacNeil didn't matter. No one minded Scot eating Scot, but what if they couldn't answer their own questions?

Not one whit abashed, Macfarlane went on: 'Weel, one even simpler. What regiment am I in?'

He looked at them grimly as if defying someone to say 'the Gordon Highlanders'.

Ransome did, and started to double round the square in the wake of MacNeil.

'Anyone, then?'

'The Royal Scots,' said Lilburne.

'Ah, gude, gude.' Macfarlane looked at Lilburne with an almost human interest. 'That's better.

'Noo as a reward I'll tell you what I'll do. If you can give me five facts about my regiment you're excused the rest of the parade.'

'Sir,' said Lilburne, 'the Royal Scots is the First of Foot, the oldest regiment in the British Army, being formed originally in the French service. Its nickname is, because of that, "Pontius Pilate's Bodyguard". Its tartan is Hunting Stewart except for the pipers, who wear Royal Stewart. Its regimental march is "Dumbarton's Drums", composer unknown, mixed with the "Daughter of the Regiment" from Donizetti's opera of the same name in honour of

Queen Victoria who was the regiment's colonel-in-chief.' He drew breath. 'There's a little couplet, "First of Foot, Right of the line, and Pride of the British Army," and, and,' he faltered, 'and the regiment raised more territorial battalions in the First World War than any other regiment. Nineteen to be precise.'

C.S.M. Macfarlane's facial expression had changed from one of deep cunning when he put the question to one of amazement when Lilburne started his recital, mixed with pride as if he were himself almost wholly responsible for his regiment's record. Now, Lilburne having come to a breathless stop, he looked at him steadily, eyeing his cavalry cap-badge.

'Aye,' he said slowly, 'quite correct. You'll have served in the regiment, Cadet, at some time?'

'No, sir.'

'Your father, perhaps?'

'No, sir.'

'Where then did you get it all?'

'From the back of a cigarette-card, sir,' said Lilburne.

Sergeant-Major Macfarlane exhaled slowly. 'Aye,' he said. 'Aye, weel, I said you could go so you'd better fall out.'

Lilburne remembered to turn to his right as smartly as possible for fear of reprisals, and marched away.

Behind him he heard a voice saying, 'Noo, for the rest of yew . . . '

The screams and yells followed him in diminishing volume as he headed for the guardroom telephone. If he was really quick he could get a bath as well.

9

WEDNESDAY morning dawned warm and misty with that curious haze that promises, in June at least, more heat to come. 'A' Company stood in shirtsleeves on a stretch of heath about five miles from Upshott. Major Hawksworth stood at an improvised table, his four captains behind him. 'You may sit down, gentlemen,' he said, 'and smoke, so long as you don't start a heath fire.'

He went on with the aid of a map to explain the three-day scheme. Broadly, the cadets were left on their own. There would be two opposing forces composed of 1 and 2 Platoons and 3 and 4 Platoons respectively. Cadets would command each in turn for twelve hours.

Each force had an allotted start-point and would advance towards each other, endeavouring to collect information or capture prisoners as a preparation for the full battle on the Friday morning. Two captains would follow each force, observing and reporting and acting as umpires. The whole action would be an infantry battle in miniature, designed to test the powers of command and leadership of the various cadets.

As Major Hawksworth spoke, rations were handed out and blank ammunition, plus allotted numbers of Bren guns and mortars.

The two forces, labelled, with that heavy facetiousness that the Army adopts on these occasions, Ruritanians and Arcadians, separated and were given their individual instructions. Arkwright, Ransome, Churchouse, and Lilburne were all Ruritanians and were given red armbands. Arcadians wore blue.

The Ruritanians, sitting on the ground, watched the Arcadians depart in a northerly direction in two troop-carrying lorries.

Captain Tunnicliffe, Lilburne's indolent gunner friend, walked over and stood among them, one hand thrust negligently in his pocket.

'Right,' he said, 'here's a marked map. Your first objective is Code-Sign Pineapple, which as you will see is not far from Pirbright.

'With the map you'll find a sheet of instructions for the force commander. These will be obeyed. How they will be obeyed is up to the force commander, who chooses his own second in command and platoon officers. Everyone in fact down to his own batman and runner.

'You'll get half an hour to do all that. I want you to move from here at'—he looked at his watch—'0900 hours.'

Captain Tunnicliffe paused, had a quick glance at the map in the plastic-covered case, and ran his finger down the typed sheet attached to it.

'Oh, there's also the wavelength for the walkie-talkies and the 88 sets.'

He looked up. 'For the first twelve hours the force commander will be Officer-Cadet MacNeil.'

Everyone bar the person named sighed with relief, they thought inaudibly.

Tunnicliffe smiled, walked away to a hammock, sat down, and began to smoke a cigarette.

MacNeil, his freckled, pinched face set, got to his feet.

Lilburne turned to Churchouse. 'God Almighty, Little Mac-Nasty himself! It'll be the most dreadful bog. I bet they've chosen him just to see if he's any sense at all.'

'They'll soon know,' said Arkwright.

'The really prize four-letter man in charge of one for twelve hours. I know he loathes me, I bet I get some filthy job.'

'We all will,' said Ransome, 'he hates us all. Especially me, ever since I was sick over his bed.'

MacNeil had finished scrutinizing the map and his appointments. 'My second in command, Parker.'

'Good old Pimply,' said Arkwright, 'he'll be some help. If he falls asleep he'll mumble unmentionable things into the wireless.'

MacNeil was coming farther down his list to those who would have no authority but merely functions.

'Bren, 1 Platoon, Churchouse. Mortar, 1 Platoon, Ransome. Signaller, 1 Platoon, Lilburne.'

Lilburne as a choice for this was reasonable enough, as he was in the R.A.C. He had qualified on wireless. The drawback was that he had to carry it. Arkwright, who had apparently escaped, forbore to say to the other three, 'I told you so.' Ransome looked mutinously at the mortar with its folding legs and a haversack full of thunderflashes for ammunition.

'Right,' said MacNeil. He too looked at his wristwatch. 'We'll move now.'

No. 1 Platoon formed up behind him. No 2 Platoon came behind Parker, who looked behind his pimples more clueless than usual.

Lilburne took up his position behind MacNeil, his 88 set strapped on his chest, his earphones over his beret, the aerial swaying and whipping as he moved.

He looked towards Cresswell, his opposite number in 2 Platoon also coping with six feet of aerial, a throat microphone, and a pair of earphones.

Lilburne winked at him. 'Won't be able to hear you in the woods so not too many complicated messages, Alec, please.'

'Right, Charles.' Cresswell turned a switch and produced a high-pitched howl from his set.

MacNeil whipped round. 'For God's sake!' he said. 'Parker and I will give you two the messages. It's up to you, you're both wireless chaps, to get them across; if you can do it in tanks surely you can do the same on foot.'

'All right, netting you know,' said Lilburne.

Cresswell removed his earphones and put his head towards MacNeil. 'What?' he said. 'Didn't hear you, on the air, you know.'

MacNeil gritted his teeth. 'Cavalry,' he muttered, and turned away. He moved his right hand in a sweeping gesture reminiscent of wagon-train bosses in Westerns and the whole cavalcade moved off. At a small birch-wood Parker's platoon separated to the left and was lost to sight.

All through the summer morning 1 Platoon trudged on through the woods of Hampshire, MacNeil at their head now and again looking importantly at his map or his compass. Lilburne marched behind him, occupying himself with hitting the leaves of each third tree with his wireless aerial. After the first mile he muttered, 'Wireless silence, I suppose,' to MacNeil.

He, not hearing or understanding properly, said, 'Of course.'

Lilburne switched off the set and marched on. Now and again he whistled bits of Beethoven happily to himself.

At the tail end of the platoon Churchouse changed the Bren from hand to hand and Ransome sweated under the mortar. He scowled ferociously at a party of hikers and itched to throw a thunderflash at a courting couple he saw recumbent on the bracken.

'All around us we see,' he said, 'people enjoying the innocent pleasures of the summer while we march along in horrible khaki carrying repulsive burdens,' he shifted the mortar round on his back, 'under the command of an idiot.'

'George, why do you think they've put him in charge? Because they think he's good or because they think he's bad?'

'Dunno. I suppose they can watch us all. Probably only put knife-edge cases in command. Last chance of proving themselves. Shouldn't be difficult. Anyone can find his way from Upshott to Pirbright by walking up the main road.'

'Yes. But we are supposed to be looking for the Arcadians.'

'—— the Arcadians. They're probably all asleep somewhere.'

'I wonder where Parker and his boys have got to,' said Churchouse. 'We didn't have an "O" Group, did you notice?'

'Parallel to us, aren't they, Nick?'

'Anyway we've got Charles and Alec Cresswell.'

'They're all right, George, both know their jobs.'

'Yes, but I wouldn't put it past either of them to play some trick or other.'

'No, I suppose not. A bit idle, both of them.'

'Tell me, Nick, what do you think of Charles?'

'Oh, he'll get through.'

'I don't mean that, as a chap.'

'Oh, charming fellow.'

'You don't think he's a bit of a snob, a stuffed shirt?'

Churchouse opened his eyes wide and stared at Ransome. 'Oh no, certainly not, why?'

'Oh, doesn't matter.'

They marched on.

Lunch was snatched from haversack rations, the cadets sitting round in a circle.

MacNeil raised his voice. 'Anyone seen anything?' he said.

'Yes,' drawled Lilburne. 'A girl being undressed by a chap in a wood and a couple of red squirrels. Girl was rather——'

'Oh, shut up.' MacNeil looked at him furiously. 'Some people don't seem to realize we've got to pull together in this thing.'

Ransome ostentatiously lit a cigarette and lay on his back. Scovington began to take an interest in his boots.

'Well,' said MacNeil, he looked round uncertainly, 'we'd better get cracking.' He stood up. The others followed him more slowly.

They marched on.

'Put a message through to Two, will you, to report progress.' MacNeil didn't bother to turn his head.

Lilburne quietly switched on his set and started to speak. 'Hello, Roger two. Hello, Roger two. Sitrep. Now, over.'

At the fourth repetition MacNeil turned to him. 'No answer?' he said.

'Nothing heard,' corrected Lilburne solemnly. 'Trees, you know, I'll try a bit more aerial.' He began to fit another two feet, nearly removing MacNeil's eye in the process.

'Hullo, Roger two. Hullo, Roger two. Are you receiving me? Over.' Lilburne shrugged his shoulders. 'Trees——' he began.

'I know, I know.' MacNeil looked at his map and strode on. The platoon fanned out as they approached a glade.

Suddenly a loud crack, followed by another—a shout.

'Down.' MacNeil gestured with his flat hand. The platoon took cover.

'Whoosh!' A lighted thunderflash whistled over their heads from the rear and disappeared into some bushes thirty yards ahead. A loud explosion followed.

'That swine Ransome and his bloody mortar,' hissed MacNeil. Lilburne tended his 88 set with a new interest.

Minutes elapsed. 'Right,' said MacNeil. He gestured with his hand. The platoon rose and doubled across the grass and into the wood beyond led by MacNeil, waving his map-board like a scimitar.

They crashed through undergrowth, their equipment clanking, and burst into another glade. MacNeil stopped, Churchouse hesitated as, unordered, he placed the Bren out to the flank to provide supporting fire.

Two schoolboys and a man in braces faced them. Both boys had air-rifles.

'Did you do that?' said the man angrily.

'Do what?' said MacNeil.

'That bleeding firework. Just missed my boy here.' He indicated the shorter and uglier of the two. 'Might ha' killed him.'

'No such luck,' said a voice too loudly from the back.

'Now, look here.' The man advanced on MacNeil.

'I'm sorry,' said MacNeil.

'I know all about you lot,' said the man, pointing at their white cadets' patches, 'training to be officers. Menace, that's what you are.'

MacNeil's temper gave way. He had had a trying day.

'This is a military exercise,' he said, spacing his words, 'and you can go to hell; shouldn't be using airguns, anyway.'

The man looked at the young soldiers now grouped automatically round their leader. He saw that all were armed. His son tugged at his arm. 'You shut up,' he said, pushing him away.

MacNeil was master of the situation and knew it. He waved his arm. The platoon moved forward. The little group of three moved to one side.

'I'll write to your C.O.,' said the man.

MacNeil ignored him.

'I'd write to my M.P. if I were you,' said Scovington as he passed. 'Much better, question in the House probably.'

'Cor,' said the short ugly boy, 'aren't we la-de-da.'

His father scowled. He stood, his fists clenched, until the tail end of the procession passed him.

'Actually, the Russians have just landed,' muttered Ransome as he sweated past with the mortar.

The platoon was in better spirits after that. Even MacNeil seemed to have grown in stature.

Their good spirits lasted until five o'clock when at what Mac-Neil decided must be Pineapple, a crossroads a mile south of Pirbright, they emerged from the woods to wait for No. 2 Platoon.

At five-thirty No. 2 Platoon, looking the worse for wear, also emerged. Captain Tunnicliffe had already arrived by road in a jeep. MacNeil and Parker stood together, a picture of two great commanders relaxing after a day's battle.

Tunnicliffe turned to them. 'Well, you're here, but you're both hellish late and why no wireless communication?'

The two great commanders looked a little crestfallen as they turned towards their black-bereted wireless operators, who stood chattering beside them.

'Trees,' said Cresswell and Lilburne simultaneously.

The rest of Wednesday evening passed uneventfully. MacNeil and Parker fussed about supervising what really needed no supervising.

The Ruritanians had an evening meal and settled down for the night. Bivouacs were pitched, guards were mounted, passwords were chosen, all in that rather unreal world that the Army always creates on manœuvres, for not a mile away could be seen a main road, illuminated and beaconed, along which cars and buses carried ordinary citizens to cinemas, pubs, and their homes.

Nevertheless at Pineapple the first sentries were posted and under the instruction of Captain Tunnicliffe MacNeil handed over his command to a serious youth called Townshend who, apart from having once stated to Cresswell that he hated horses, had made little mark on 'A' Company. He chose Vorontsoff, the cadet of White Russian ancestry, as his second in command and together they began to walk self-importantly round the perimeter of the tiny camp.

If one closed one's eyes to the lighted highway the picture was of a military encampment anywhere, at any time. Cadets in their shirtsleeves wandered about with blankets, others squatted on the ground and checked their weapons. The outlines blurred by the fading light, the picture irresistibly reminded one of those illustrations much favoured by the *Illustrated London News* at the turn of the century. It could have been some scene on the South African veldt—a youthful Winston Churchill and a voice singing 'Dolly Gray' would have made the illusion complete.

Lilburne lay luxuriously on the ground, still warm from the sun, and tried somewhat unsuccessfully to drink from a large mug of tea resting on his chest. Churchouse sat rather uncomfortably on a pile of blankets and smoked a cigarette.

'Funny, Nick. I wonder what real fighting is like. Do you think it's absolute chaos?'

'Well, I suppose it's a matter of little actions all over the place, really, but of course in the war there was a much better organization.'

'Oh, I don't know, people were on their own in Burma and the desert. Infantry, anyhow.'

'I admit that and I suppose they always get the worst of it. In armoured regiments as you are always moving I suppose you get a bigger picture of what's going on.'

'Yes, and you don't have to live literally on the ground all the time.'

'Yet I suppose even if one were in the infantry this is what one would remember; lying back at the end of the day, and forget the rest.'

'Oh, I know that, Nick. No one says they hated the war. Everyone seems to have enjoyed it, even when they say it was absolute hell with a sort of relish.'

'Perhaps, Charles, it's all some sort of psychological defence mechanism. One only remembers the pleasant parts and forgets the rest.'

'Might be it. It might also be a reason why wars start again. Not enough people remember the hell of the last one.'

Lilburne stirred himself. 'Cigarette?'

Churchouse threw him one.

Lilburne, lighting it, smiled. 'We seem to be getting very philosophical just because we're sleeping in a field. After all, we must remember that the Commandant said, "We're all hired killers." If we talk about the hell of war that great militarist MacNeil might think we're not pulling our weight.'

'Doesn't matter, Charles. Townshend is O.C. tonight.'

'Yes, I know. By the way, why aren't either of us doing guard?'

Churchouse looked a bit embarrassed. 'Well, Vorontsoff and I had a word.'

'A get-together of the old Imperialist officer corps, you mean?'

From anyone other than Lilburne the remark would have offended Churchouse.

'Yes, we clicked heels at each other and he thought that, as we had had the heavy jobs today . . .'

'Well, splendid. I'm glad my name was included, or rather, as Sam Goldwyn said, included out.'

Churchouse smiled. 'Of course I had to say your mother was a Polish countess who had been a friend of the Czar's.'

Lilburne, still lying down, clicked his boot heels together and saluted.

'*Danke schön, Excellenz.*'

He stretched out again and lay back. It really was almost pleasant to be alive.

'I suppose, Charles, it's the old brick-wall principle. It's pleasant when you stop. I must say I'm looking forward to my few days' leave, though I do rather dread the next bit afterwards.'

'Oh, nonsense.' Churchouse worried far too much about his abilities, Lilburne thought privately, or more precisely tended to put into words what everyone else left unsaid.

'Look, Nick. Navigation, lesson one. There's the North Star and the Plough.' He pointed upwards.

Churchouse followed his arm. The dusk was deepening, throwing the stars into relief.

'Funny to think that they have been looking down for centuries on people.'

Ransome's figure loomed up.

'Have you got any blankets?' He noticed Churchouse's improvised couch. 'For God's sake, Nick, you've got enough for a company there.' He tugged at two.

Churchouse, uncomplaining, allowed him to take them away. He shrugged his shoulders.

'*Midsummer Night's Dream.* Enter Bottom.'

Lilburne began to arrange his blankets. 'Better turn in. Who knows what hell tomorrow will hold.'

'Good night, Charles.'

'Good night, Nick.'

Both lay down and arranged themselves, trying to make their bodies conform to the hollows of the ground.

Lilburne watched while Churchouse lit another cigarette. He watched its glowing end until he fell asleep. Churchouse smoked on, looking up at the Plough, and Orion with his belt and sword lower down towards the horizon.

A few yards off a sentry walked his rounds and farther away in the woods a hunting owl screeched twice and was silent.

10

ON THURSDAY morning the command for that day was given to Lloyd, who looked stunned at the news and proceeded to read his orders and try to look at his map at the same time.

'You see,' said Lilburne to Ransome, 'they obviously choose the doubtful ones. We were right. This is their way of making or breaking those they think aren't quite up to scratch.'

'At that rate, Charles, I'll be next.'

'Nonsense, George, only the real dregs.'

Arkwright joined them. 'In for a lovely day today, you lucky lads, with the Idiot Boy himself in charge. First we get MacNasty, then that drip Townshend, and now that marvel of co-ordination between muscle and mind, the Body Beautiful, the P.T.I.'s dream, Mr. Neanderthal of 1955.'

'I know,' said Lilburne, 'just what we were saying. This whole thing is just done to try out the doubtful ones, the potential failures. You agree, don't you, George?'

Ransome looked at Lilburne but said nothing.

'The only trouble,' said Arkwright, 'is that one just has to trudge along doing what these goons say.'

'Not to worry. Pleasant country walk. Could be worse.'

Ransome looked at both of them and wondered if they had any right to be so self-confident. He himself secretly dreaded being picked to command that night, the night of the battle.

Arkwright turned to him. 'I wonder, George, who'll be in

charge tonight? If it's anyone as stupid as Lloyd it really could be a shambles.'

Lilburne laughed. 'Oh, tonight will go to the most doubtful of all; for him the emergency, the real test.' He adopted a Blimpish voice and stroked an imaginary moustache. 'Show what the fellah's really made of. Surprisin', ye know, what a real show brings out in chaps. Knew a chap on the Frontier once, '06 I think it was——'

'One Platoon fall in,' shouted Lloyd, rather despairingly.

Despite Lilburne's prognostications of disaster the day went well.

Lloyd, obviously trying very hard, had his 'O' Group. He explained his plan and gave his orders concisely and sensibly.

The approach march and the reconnaissances went well, perhaps because everyone really liked Lloyd and did their best for him out of a mixture of affection and sympathy, and one had to admit that under the stress of circumstance the company buffoon did obviously make efforts. His foot drill might be poor, his P.T. clumsy, and his intelligence not of the most incisive, but he could, when in command, persuade others to do what he wanted. Consequently, for those like Lilburne and Ransome, with no special tasks, the day passed pleasantly enough. They marched again through the peaceful, pleasant woods, but this time their various tasks of reconnaissance and reporting were tinged with some excitement as their enemy the Arcadians were within striking distance.

It was in the afternoon as they marched together that Ransome asked Lilburne to come to a party over the coming weekend. He never really knew why he did it; he wasn't all that fond of Lilburne, whom he was quite sure would not mix well with his own friends in Hampstead. He wondered really if he had done it only to break into the constant conversations Lilburne had with Cresswell, also in their section, about people Ransome had never heard of. They had chattered on for the best part of the hour after lunch in what Ransome considered upper-class voices about weekends here and parties there when, as much to show Cresswell, whom he disliked, that he too could compete in the social sphere, Ransome said quite casually: 'I wonder, Charles, if you would like to come to a party on Saturday evening if you're in London? Probably an all-night affair.'

'Certainly, George, love to. We must exchange telephone numbers. Perhaps I can give you a lift.' Ransome wondered how Lilburne knew he hadn't a car, or perhaps he just assumed it, but they talked on, making plans, and Cresswell dropped back. Ransome had scored his victory, he had now got Lilburne to himself. As for the victim, he spent some time afterwards wondering why he had accepted. He was quite sure that he would not like Ransome's friends very much. Finally he justified it all by assuring himself that he had accepted only out of kindness to George. In fact Lilburne, like many essentially lonely people, could never refuse an invitation.

The Ruritanians were now moving in an easterly direction towards Ash Vale, where Lloyd had decided the Arcadians must be. Both forces had carried out minor tasks, but it was not until now in the late afternoon that any real chance of contact arose. This of course had been deliberately planned by the instructors when preparing the orders handed to each successive commander. Thursday night was to be devoted to a night exercise and an eventual battle.

By five o'clock the Ruritanians had reached one of the boundaries of their area, the London–Upshott railway line. Here, following his instructions, Lloyd gave orders to halt and rest. Captain Tunnicliffe arrived with the other instructors in a jeep followed by a more welcome sight—a 15 cwt. containing tea-urns and rations.

The cadets, tired by their exertions and the heat, sank thankfully to the ground with sandwiches and mugs of tea. Cresswell and Arkwright put themselves down beside Lilburne.

'Christ, Charles, hope it's not some vigorous bastard who's

put in command tonight. I'm absolutely out,' said Cresswell.

Captain Tunnicliffe walked over to them. 'Oh, Lilburne, you are to take over when this meal is finished. I'll give you all the gen now.'

Lilburne gaped at him and stood up. 'Yes, sir.' He added, quite unnecessarily, 'Right.' He accepted a map-board and a typed sheet of orders.

'I shall be over there with my fellow instructors,' went on Tunnicliffe, pointing to a small hut that was being erected. 'Don't blow us out of our beds.' He smiled and wandered off.

Lilburne and Arkwright looked at each other. Arkwright found his voice first. 'You may be a bastard but I don't think even Alec here would call you vigorous.'

Lilburne's mind in those few seconds had been turning somersaults. Was he himself in danger of being chucked out? Did they think he was a 'knife-edge case'? What had he done wrong? Night exercises were tricky anyhow, anything might go wrong through no fault of his own.

By God, he'd have to do his best!

This rather vague resolve made, his usual air of nonchalance returned.

'My dear chap,' he said to Arkwright, 'I've obviously been chosen so that our instructors can get some sleep, but we'll see.'

He walked off towards the tea-urn.

The other cadets looked at him carrying his map-case and papers.

'Make way,' said Ransome, 'for Knife-edge Lilburne.'

Lilburne ignored him, and looked at his watch without seeing the time.

'O.K.,' he said, 'I'll give out my appointments in figures five minutes,' he had consciously adopted the curious speech of R.A.C. wireless procedure, 'and then call an "O" Group.'

He looked round unsmiling; if he had to do this act he might as well do it well.

He chose his appointments carefully, second in command, Churchouse, who apart from being a personal friend was by far the most efficient soldier in the company.

'No. 1 Platoon Commander Carter, and No. 2 Platoon Commander Drysdale.' Both popular, extraordinarily tough rugger players who would quite cheerfully carry out almost any task imposed on them.

Wireless Operator Arkwright, as efficient as any, and finally Cresswell as batman and runner, because the job was a sinecure and he might as well have somebody to talk to.

At the 'O' Group, which he carried out with a dead-straight face entirely according to the book, going through the laid-down procedure of Intention, Method, Own Troops, Enemy, etc., he sprang one surprise. 'John.' He turned towards Meynell, a cadet he privately loathed as being loud and hearty. 'John,' he said, 'it is quite obvious that the other side will be mounting an attack against our main position here to take place either during the night or at dawn. To do that the first thing they've got to do is find out our position and then do a recce. What we must do is harass them so much during the night that firstly they don't find out where we are and secondly they're never left in peace to do any planning.'

Meynell nodded in agreement and cautiously said, 'Yes.'

'That's going to be your job, John,' said Lilburne. 'I want you to pick twenty toughs,' he smiled, 'to go out on a patrol and find out as much as you can. Get that back to me and give 'em hell as often as possible.

'After this "O" Group collect your twenty bodies, get yourselves into suitable kit, blacken your faces, and report to me at 0830.'

Meynell nodded again and opened his mouth to speak.

'Right,' said Lilburne, 'now for the rest of you.' He continued with his orders. The basic plan was simple; apart from the idea of Meynell leading a harassing force, Lilburne was going to stay put. Knowing his fellow cadets he was certain that the Arcadian commander, whoever he might be, would endeavour to put up some show of aggressive spirit, if only to impress the umpires. The task of Meynell's force would be to find out what the enemy was doing, and the rest of the company would prepare a strong defensive position which could be designed as a trap for any attackers.

Lilburne issued passwords. He chose 'Helen of Troy' and 'Odysseus' for no particular reason, and gave out various combinations of Very signals. Finally he asked the question laid down by protocol and familiar to all from countless films.

'Any questions, gentlemen?'

'Yes. About sleeping arrangements,' said Townshend.

'Not necessary,' said Lilburne sharply. 'No one will get any.' He was amazed that no one said anything. No one laughed. Apparently they all took it quite seriously and accepted his orders.

He stood up and again looked at his watch. 'Meynell's group back here at 0830. The rest of you, move.'

He left them sorting themselves out and walked over to the instructors' tent to explain, as was expected, his plans to Captain Tunnicliffe.

He greeted him with a smile and offered him a camp-stool. Lilburne outlined his plan, wondering all the while how many times Tunnicliffe himself had done this sort of thing in the past in a real war, dealing with men's lives and dealing with real wounds and death. How could he take this Boy Scout charade seriously? thought Lilburne.

Apparently, though, he did, for he accepted the plan gravely enough and only said at the end: 'Bit out of character all this activity, isn't it? What about sleep?'

Lilburne smiled but without, he hoped, relaxing his expression of determination. 'I am afraid not many people are going to get much, sir, least of all, I hope, the enemy.'

Tunnicliffe shrugged his shoulders. 'Would you like a glass of whisky?' He reached for a bottle and some glasses inside the tent.

Lilburne had a moment of indecision and played his master stroke.

'No, thank you, sir, I must get back to give a quick briefing to Meynell's chaps before they go out.' He saluted and walked to his H.Q. He looked at cadets digging weapon-pits and fox-holes. He was very pleased with himself. His briefing of Meynell and his chosen twenty, wearing pullovers and P.T. shoes and with their faces stained with mud and cocoa, would have done credit to Field Marshal Montgomery or Mr. Jack Hawkins.

Even Meynell looked impressed, and indeed smiled with a sort of soldierly understanding when Lilburne concluded by saying: 'When you find the enemy I leave it to you. You'll be able to form your own plans then, you'll be the chap on the spot. So long, however,' he added, 'as someone gets back to me with the information I want.'

Meynell's small command moved off cautiously, nearly invisible in the gathering darkness; a whispering of orders and they had disappeared.

Lilburne sat on the edge of his own trench, for the night his command post. Cresswell was sorting out blankets and weapons. He handed Lilburne a Very pistol and some cartridges.

Arkwright fiddled with his wireless set. Churchouse appeared suddenly from behind a nearby tree.

'The outer line is O.K., Charles.' He pointed out the direction in which he had sited various outlying sentries, well dug in and camouflaged.

'The reliefs are O.K. and everyone has their orders about reporting activity.'

'Splendid, Nick,' said Lilburne. 'I should get a bit of sleep now if you can. I'll wake you if you're needed.' Lilburne sat on musing to himself. He wondered how much of an act his performance was. Perhaps in real battles everyone had to put on an act. Could one ever really tell if one was sincere or not? One part of him said, 'This is what I must do to make this thing a success,' and the other looked over his shoulder, as it were, and said, 'Charles, you're a bogus devil, but don't think you're kidding everybody.'

He remembered a character study he had once read of Disraeli, who it was said preserved an outward show of good humour and cynicism to cloak a deep intensity of purpose and a genuine sincerity. Yet in all men it had been said there was layer upon layer of conflicting characteristics, the scoffer concealed the idealist and under that another layer perhaps of humour and further down—no one really knew what the real character was, least of all the person himself. Perhaps it didn't matter. Lilburne didn't know. He shook himself, looked round at the shadows of bushes and trees, and joined the others in the trench. He rested his elbows on the edge and, perhaps still acting the great commander oppressed by his thoughts, lit a cigarette. He remembered his security too late and held the burning end below the parapet.

A roar and a flash and a lighted train went by, not fifty yards away, on its way to London.

Arkwright stirred. 'Charles,' he said, 'don't you wish you were on that instead of in a hole in the ground?'

While the law-abiding and civilian slept, 'A' Company, divided for the moment into Ruritanians and Arcadians, tried hard to keep its eyes open.

It was easy for Meynell and his task force, who made their way through the birch-woods transformed by the night into a semi-tropical forest, as novels used to say, full of hidden menace. Not one of the twenty-one cadets, Meynell included, stolid and tough though he was, did not imagine himself on some greater, more dangerous, mission. The night has a great power to let loose our imaginations and even prompt our actions, as Lady Macbeth well knew.

As they moved stealthily together, searching with their eyes for a hidden enemy, their senses alerted by some automatic atavistic instinct, these young men could not but let some parts of their thoughts wander, tinging their every action with an importance and a dangerous reality impossible to maintain during the day.

Meynell was himself in some Hentyish fantasy, he had already killed thirty of the enemy with a Commando knife to earn the third bar to his M.C., when he was brought back to reality by nearly blundering into a small tent, obviously that of the umpires attached to the Arcadian force.

His logic after that was Napoleonic in its simplicity—the Arcadians themselves must be near at hand. His followers were given swift whispered orders and disappeared in various directions in groups of three.

It was easy for Pimply Parker, the commander of but a day ago, now the farthermost right-flank outpost of Lilburne's force. He had been ordered by Churchouse to watch a small road which curved into the wood on their right, forming an obvious line which an attacking enemy would have to cross. Originally Churchouse had simply told him to find a good position and dig himself in, but on returning conscientiously half an hour later had found Parker on the outer edge of the road looking inwards. With some heat Churchouse had pointed out the inadequacies of Parker as a tactician and then indicated a point on the inner edge of the road commanding an excellent view, where Parker was to dig himself in.

This he had done—for he was frightened of Churchouse and of a bad report—almost up to the neck. He was completely concealed and he could see. Admittedly he could do very little else, but that didn't worry him until midnight.

At that witching hour he was nearly blinded by the headlights of an open sports car that came towards him; for a dreadful moment he thought it was going to run over his head. He was about to shout out when it came to rest off the road with its running-board about six feet from his nose and his concealing screen of bushes.

The engine was switched off and then the lights. He heard and half saw a man and a woman transfer themselves to the back seat. There they moved into each other's arms, the man lit two cigarettes, and in low voices they talked.

Parker, fascinated, unable to move, listened to the conversation of these two heads, disembodied by the car door.

They were not two adolescent love-birds pausing for a pecked kiss before the inevitable return to their respective parents. Their voices, both in accent and tone, soon revealed these two as being nearer thirty than twenty and of what Parker, who read too many gossip columns, secretly thought of as smart café society.

The cigarettes gleamed red and Parker, listening to their conversation, learned that they were not husband and wife but the husband and wife of two other people.

For a moment he had a blush-making vision of himself giving evidence in the divorce courts. 'Peeress's Counsel Cross-examines Cadet' flashed through his mind as a staring headline, and he tried to close his eyes and his ears. He failed.

The two burning cigarette ends, one after the other, arced into the darkness. The second fell short of the first.

Parker sank his head in his shoulders and toyed with the idea of firing his rifle with its charge of blank to follow the cigarette ends.

Conversation from the car dropped to desultory mutterings and whispers and once a female giggle.

A light-coloured blouse appeared and the woman's voice said urgently, 'Darling, you don't need your coat.'

The next hour or so can be imagined. Parker himself had little need to do so; what little was lost to his view by the intervention of the car door he found easy to supplement, torn as he was between embarrassment and lustful curiosity.

After a considerable gap conversation resumed. Cigarettes were again lit. Parker felt in need of one himself.

'God, it's two o'clock! I must get back,' said the man's voice.

A door opened and with a flash of legs the woman slid out of her seat. In her hand she had her skirt. She pulled her blouse over the door of the car. She wrapped her skirt around her, she thrust her arms into her blouse, she danced a small jig as she adjusted her stockings and shoes. They had high heels which sank into the turf. Parker could with a stretch have closed his hands over her ankles. He thought about this.

She got back into the car, the front this time. The man joined her. The lights went on, the engine fired. 'If Richard ever finds out,' said the woman.

'Oh, really!' said the man, 'you'd think there were spies hiding in the bushes.'

The clutch was let in, the car moved on to the road and rapidly became two red eyes disappearing in the distance.

It was easy too for Fletcher, the commander of the Arcadians.

At one o'clock he began an 'O' Group for a night sortie rather similar to that planned by Lilburne with Meynell's force. At this friendly little conference Fletcher, who had been unwise enough to choose his friends as subordinate commanders, was interrupted by the news that two of his scouts had disappeared, leaving only their boots behind.

Before he had fully digested the import of this an unholy yelling broke out some fifty yards away and then the sound of rifles and thunderflashes.

Fletcher arrived as the last thunderflash fizzed out at the bottom of a trench.

He re-aligned his outer defence ring and returned to his 'O' Group. His harrying force went out into the night, ill prepared and hurried. They returned in two groups an hour or two later having accomplished nothing.

But by then Fletcher didn't care, he had other things to occupy his mind; his second in command had been hit in the face by a clod of earth that had whistled out of the night and a Bren-gun had disappeared when blankets had been thrown over the heads of its two-man crew.

Incidents such as these continued. Meynell was enjoying himself in the darkness. Fletcher was not. By two o'clock in the morning he had decided to concentrate on a dawn frontal attack of the simplest kind. When he was not cursing the other side and seeing himself returned to his unit, he was promising himself a wonderful uninterrupted sleep on some other night.

For those who were actively engaged, voluntarily or against their will, it was easy to keep awake; for those with little or nothing to do it was difficult.

Lilburne leaned on the parapet of his trench and tried to keep sleep at bay with constant cigarettes. Below him Cresswell slept, and snored unashamedly. Arkwright was in the shadows and could not be seen clearly. His back was against the end of the trench, his wireless set was beside him, but it had not been in use and he had not spoken for over an hour.

It was only when the ever-active Churchouse returned after doing his rounds inspecting sentries that Lilburne shook himself into complete wakefulness. He shifted his beret on his head and rubbed his eyes and tried to penetrate the surrounding darkness. Churchouse stood beside him and they talked in whispers. It was thus they were seen by Meynell, who half crawled and half ran towards them.

'Splendid, Charles,' he said breathlessly, diving into the trench beside them. He looked down and kicked Cresswell's boot-soles. 'Got a few presents for you.'

'What about the Arcadians' position, John?'

Meynell told him, tersely; he broke off. 'Ah, here they come.'

Lilburne stared into the night.

Five or six cadets came towards the trench. They pulled and dragged between them two others.

'We got these two, stripped off their boots, and brought them along,' said Meynell.

Lilburne looked at them.

'Look here, Charles, what's the bloody idea? This is only an exercise,' said one.

'Shut up,' said Meynell.

Lilburne was still wondering about the boots. 'Right,' said Meynell, 'tie 'em up, arms and feet, and stick 'em down here.' He indicated the bottom of the trench. This was done amidst protests.

'I think . . .' began Lilburne.

'Shall we go back, Charles? I've got an idea we might be able to——'

'Yes, John, I think you had better, but keep me in the picture and be back here an hour before dawn.'

Meynell and his five companions disappeared.

Lilburne resumed his place in the trench. He looked down at the prisoners ranged beside Cresswell. All three were asleep. Churchouse moved to look at the captured Bren-gun and sat down beside it. Lilburne wrapped a blanket round his shoulders, propped up his head on his elbows, and continued to look at the night.

11

THE morning came up hazily through the beech-woods and contained a promise of more sun to come.

The Ruritanians, rubbing their eyes and stretching as Churchouse made his last-minute rounds, were awake just in time to hear crashing through the undergrowth the noise of Fletcher's Arcadians.

On they came, shouting and cheering, firing their rifles as soon as they thought they saw the Ruritanian positions. Lilburne, still with his blanket round his shoulders, waited until they were almost upon him.

'Fire!' he shouted.

A crackle of blank ammunition and the bang of thunderflashes came up from the slit trenches.

None of the Arcadians, of course, fell to the ground. They simply galloped and gambolled, large overgrown English school-boys, enjoying themselves. Nevertheless, the point was obvious. Fletcher had led them straight into a horseshoe-shaped trap. In real warfare Lilburne's force, without exposing themselves, would have massacred them.

Still, this was a morning in a Hampshire wood, the sun was beginning to shine, and the only ammunition was blank. Cheerful free-for-alls developed among cadets who refused to fall down and die because an unloaded Bren-gun had been waved in their direction. Lilburne alone did not join in, perhaps because he had not slept at all. All night he had stayed huddled in his blanket; he was now rather disappointed that his victory, which was so complete, would not be signalized in some way. For a moment he wished they had been armed with live ammunition.

Arkwright stood up and put his American-style Armoured Corps helmet on his head. All around Arcadians cheerfully wrestled with Ruritanians.

He picked up his wireless set. 'This is the battle film to end all battle films,' he intoned, in a nasal American accent.

'It tells the story of the men of the U.S. Marine Corps who fought on the beaches at Okinawa and of the women who fought with them. Their commander,' he waved a hand at Lilburne, 'Colonel G. Hamburger, is a bastard. You'll hate him. Everyone in the film is a bastard; they're all tough, hard, lean, and relentless. You'll hate them all.

'Every part is played by an actor who is himself a bastard. This is a film you just have to see. There isn't a decent character in it.'

'Get off the air, you bloody fool!' Captain Tunnicliffe appeared round the edge of his tent.

He strode towards Arkwright. The horseplay stopped, the cadets stood in small groups, embarrassed. 'I was trying to report back that the exercise was finished,' he said. 'Major Hawksworth got all that rot instead.'

He looked at Lilburne. 'Well, have you finished?' he said. 'What about a signal?'

Lilburne silently fitted a green cartridge into his Very pistol and fired it above his head.

The cartridge exploded high up, almost invisible against the blue sky.

'You and Arkwright might try to realize that there are some other qualities required of an officer other than a sense of humour,' Tunnicliffe said; his drawl had almost disappeared.

He turned on his heel and nearly cannoned into Fletcher.

'Your attack was a fiasco,' he snapped and stalked off to his tent.

Breakfast was a meal of hard-boiled eggs and slices of bread-and-butter, eaten with dirty fingers and washed down with tea from mugs which immediately afterwards served as containers for shaving water.

The cadets stood around scraping at their chins and squinting into scraps of mirror.

Cresswell and Lilburne noticed the driving-mirrors on Tunnicliffe's jeep, and with their mugs filled with lather walked across to it.

They took a mirror apiece, both looked at grey, dirty, stubbled chins above dirty khaki battledress and began to shave.

Tunnicliffe came out of his tent and started to stow his kit in the back.

'Awful,' he said, smiling, 'like the morning after.'

There didn't seem to be anything to say.

He looked at Lilburne. 'You remind me of my battery commander,' he said.

'Cheerful chap, it was right at the end of the war. I can see it now. An apple orchard in Normandy, he was shaving in a driving-mirror, I'd just finished. The sun was shining. He turned to me and said: "You know, the war's nearly over. It's grand to be alive on a day like this." I left him and a minute later a German 88 came down just where he was standing. Nothing left, just a hole in the ground. It was the only one that day.'

'Oh,' said Cresswell.

'Yes,' said Lilburne, simultaneously.

They both went on shaving; again there didn't seem to be anything to say.

Shaved, 'A' Company fell in for their return to Upshott. The exercise was over. They had to march a few miles, admittedly, to their pick-up point, and they were all grubby and dog-tired, but the rest was easy. They could relax. Those who had held command were relieved to relinquish it, and those who had not were relieved to have avoided it. Some like Fletcher were not too happy about their performance, but still the exercise was over. They fell in cheerfully on the main road, their rifles slung, their tin helmets hooked on their packs, their berets carelessly resumed. Scovington, perhaps because he was a peer, perhaps because he was in the Grenadier Guards, was put in charge and, marching at ease, they set off. None of them bothered to wonder why they had to march five miles before they were picked up. They were all tired and the troop-carriers could have met them on this part of the road as well as any other. Perhaps because they were tired, or perhaps because they were relieved, they didn't care.

They might be doing this only to fill in a morning otherwise unoccupied or it might be another more subtle test, yet there was a faint feeling of achievement and satisfaction in marching through sleepy villages and being stared at by their inhabitants. Most of the cadets tried to look like battle-scarred veterans, careless but tough.

Their destination was a small town just south of Ash Vale, which has a name quite discernible from the signposts and the A.A. book but which was overmarked on their maps for the purpose of the exercise as 'Teapot'.

'Teapot', then, is a normal overgrown village-cum-town, typical of the area, with a conventional population unstirred save by Test matches and General Elections. Unstirred that is until the morning of Friday, May the 13th. At about twelve noon 'A' Company, dusty and careless, came swinging into the tiny High Street, manœuvred its way through the traffic, and halted noisily by the war memorial on its circle of flowered green. Scovington, as his last duty of the day, screamed, 'Fall out,' in his best Caterham manner, and the cadets, their sleepless night now taking its toll, wearily and gratefully leant themselves against a neighbouring church wall.

So they waited for the arrival of their transport, gracefully accepting the stares of young children and old ladies. Some moved off into neighbouring shops for cigarettes, with the buccaneering air of men who had seen action.

The first cadet actually to sit down in the gutter was probably Ransome, others followed suit, and soon all were sitting on the pavement or edge of the war memorial green. Dirty and tired, what did it matter? Many nodded half asleep. 'Teapot's' passing population looked at them sympathetically. Parker rested his rifle carelessly against the wall and started to talk to a white-overalled girl from a sweetshop.

Two troop-carriers whined into the town and pulled up by the church; the cadets stirred lazily but didn't get up. Down from the cab of the first troop-carrier leapt Sergeant-Major Dickens, his boots gleaming, his battledress pressed, and his brasses winking. His pace-stick was under his arm in a flash. He stalked across to the reclining group. 'Get on your feet!' he yelled. The shopping crowd looked at him in amazement.

The cadets shambled to their feet, Parker's rifle crashed to the ground.

'My Gawd!' breathed Dickens. 'Who's in command?' he hissed.

'Sir!' Scovington crashed his heels to the ground and marched towards him.

Sergeant-Major Dickens was not unconscious of his large interested civilian audience, though not by a flicker of an eyelid did he show it.

His back arched, his voice rang out, 'Officer-Cadet the Viscount Scovington, sir, you are bloody idle.'

Scovington's face went a bright pink as he stood rigidly to attention.

'Look at 'em,' Dickens screamed, 'a day out in the country and what do I find? Cadets hoping to be officers lying about, collars undone, weapons thrown about,' his voice rose, 'in the gutter.' The cadets, who had shuffled themselves into positions of attention, looked at him dumbly.

'Christ, gentlemen, I've got a good mind to double you up and down this street until you're really tired!'

An outer circle of civilian faces watched him unbelievingly.

'Now,' shouted Dickens, 'fall in here.' He pointed with his pace-stick.

Three lines formed with a shuffling and a crash.

'Right dress.' More shuffling. 'Eyes front.' The cadets' faces swivelled back to look again at their tormentor.

'Right turn. Quick march.'

'A' Company marched to the lorries. Apparently the doubling threat was not to be implemented. The crowd broke up. Men shrugged their shoulders at one another and women who were mothers made private resolutions that their sons would not be soldiers. 'A' Company marched on, Sergeant-Major Dickens yelling the while, 'Left, right, heads up; swing yer arms back, they'll come forward natural.'

Most of the passers-by began to go about their normal business, but some still stared fascinated.

'A' Company halted with a bang and turned to its right, Sergeant-Major Dickens still keeping up his commentary.

'Now into those troop-carriers in sections. The last man in gets extra drill,' he yelled.

Well-mannered civilians averted their eyes—all that is save one —as the cadets scrambled into the carriers, almost treading on one another's hands in their haste. A small round-faced girl with pig-tails ran up to the erect shining figure of Sergeant-Major Dickens and, before her mother could catch her, looked up into his tight-lipped face and said piercingly, 'Horrid, nasty old man.'

The carriers revved up. Sergeant-Major Dickens who, dis-tracted, had failed to take the name of the last cadet, waited until the second was just moving and pulled himself smartly into the seat beside the driver. He cast a glance towards the crowd in time to receive the baleful glare of the small girl extending her tongue at him. Sergeant-Major Dickens gripped his pace-stick and forced himself to look at the road ahead.

The afternoon had been taken up by two occupations: one

pleasant, bathing; the other unpleasant, signing reports. Typically, the authorities had decreed that one half of 'A' Company should wash itself while the others read the reports of their six weeks, then the unwashed, cheered or depressed as the case might be by what they had read, changed places with the washed, who then went to read their reports in the company office.

Eventually, both washed and reported on, the cadets returned to their barrack rooms and enjoyed the pleasure of changing unhurriedly for their dinner that night. Luxuriously they wandered about, putting on their best battledresses without belts and with shoes instead of boots and gaiters. Cresswell and Lilburne produced the light-cream, almost white, soft shirts affected by cavalry officers which they had not been allowed to wear on parade. Churchouse toyed with a fine watchchain across his chest, but decided against it and pocketed a cigarette-holder and a swizzle-stick instead. Ransome managed to borrow a pair of clean socks from one fellow cadet and a collar-stud from another and joined them, trying to plaster down his unruly hair with water. Cresswell took one look at him and ostentatiously began to apply an expensive-looking hair lotion out of a gold-stoppered bottle.

'What did your report say, George?'

'Well, Alec, it wasn't too bad; said I lacked co-ordination but that I tried hard.'

'How ghastly!' Cresswell began to adjust his tie.

Ransome scowled but rallied. 'What was yours, then?'

'Well, it wasn't too bad. Said I was a bit careless. Still, reports don't matter a damn.'

'Mine was grossly inaccurate,' said Churchouse seriously; 'it said I was coldly efficient.'

The others looked at his solemn face and began to laugh.

'But so you are,' said Lilburne. 'A positive military maniac.'

'Reading books on strategy and polishing your boots with the spare hand,' said Cresswell. 'Quite terrifying to idle devils like me.'

'*Ihr Racker wollt ihr ewig leben?*' said Lilburne. 'I can see you saying that without any difficulty.'

Churchouse smiled.

'What's that, Charles?' said Ransome.

'Frederick the Great said it to his Guards when they hesitated in battle. Roughly, "Dogs, do you want to live for ever?" Encouraging, don't you think? It was at Kolin, wasn't it?'

'Right, Charles,' said Churchouse.

'Intellectual bastards,' said Cresswell. 'By the way, Charles, what was in your report?'

Lilburne assumed his air of indifference. 'Oh, usual stuff, said I was all right in an emergency, but otherwise lazy. Can't see how they can tell.'

What he didn't say was that his report had been rather surprisingly uncomplimentary until the last sentence, which had obviously been written in recently. It read: 'Despite his apparent casualness proves himself in an emergency.'

Obviously the night exercise had saved him. He had indeed been a knife-edge case himself.

When he had read it he had looked at Tunnicliffe, who had grimaced. 'It's not too bad, you know. Let's face it, you are a bit of a slug, you've had to be driven.'

Lilburne had privately resolved to drop the nonchalant act a bit, obviously some people could believe in it. In future he would have to take a grip on himself.

The conversation changed; someone shouted, 'Christ, it's nearly seven!' Cadets began to hurry and some to leave the barrack room for the company office where they were to board a coach hired for the occasion. Despite his new resolutions Lilburne was the last to get in, deliberately slowing to a casual walk when shouted at to hurry up by those already inside.

When the cadets reached the Clarendon Hotel they found their instructors in blues already standing at the bar. Major Hawksworth was acting as host; he smiled like Napoleon III at a gala night at the Paris opera and bought drinks all round. Churchouse found himself talking to the drill adjutant, far less romantic in blues than khaki and breeches, and revealed without his hat as being prematurely grey. Talk at the bar inevitably, after the few tentative, embarrassed starts and stops, turned to the last war.

Hawksworth was talking of a Japanese prisoner-of-war camp. 'Took everything away but my shirt and trousers but I soon made myself a badge out of wire and bits of cloth. . . .'

'Take off my hat to the Indians,' said a captain in the Seaforths. 'Those Punjabis went straight in, lost hundreds.'

'Odd chap with my brigade. Lancashire Fusiliers,' said Tunnicliffe, 'never used anything but hand-grenades, used to chuck 'em about like cricket balls. Saw him once just after Cassino . . .'

'Fellow I knew was doing brigade major when an Italian girl . . .'

'He was quite tight most of the time. . . .'

'So the sergeant-major, splendid chap, turned to me and said . . .'

'Got an M.C., I believe, gone back to being a schoolmaster in the Highlands. . . .'

'About twenty of them, blown to bits. . . .'

'Everyone knows he was queer as a coot, but lots of those types were. . . .'

'Of course, whole thing was a fiasco. . . .'

'Those S.S. chaps, only about eighteen, just left school. . . .'

'Damned good C.O. Tank burned up completely. . . .'

'And there was this Belgian major, stark naked except for his boots . . .'

The conversation, enlivened by alcohol, swirled and eddied, the cadets relaxed and warmed in the glow. Ransome began to grow red in the face. Lilburne essayed a funny story.

Arkwright quietly sipped at a pint of beer. War and death, he thought, that and a little smut seemed to be all that they could talk about and yet he realized these men, their instructors, had themselves faced dangers and made decisions, killed the enemy, and seen their own men get killed and wounded, and now they were all standing in a Hampshire hotel enjoying themselves. Perhaps they thought of themselves as just rather lucky. Those who had died could really have been very little different from those who had survived. Arkwright took a deep drink of his beer and moved over to talk to Scovington.

Sergeant-Major Dickens and the three sergeants slipped in almost unobserved and accepted pints of beer. Dickens grinned good-humouredly at Lilburne. He looked at his glass. 'Spirits,' he said, 'they'll kill you, you know, in the end.

'Captain I knew,' he said, 'in the regiment just before Alamein, it was, took a bottle of gin and . . .'

The drill adjutant moved by, a large gin-and-tonic in his hand. 'Splendid story I heard the other day,' he said to Townshend, 'about a lion-tamer who lost his nerve, so the chap who ran the circus thought he'd shame him back to work.'

Lilburne listened with half an ear.

'Brought in a female lion-tamer, terribly attractive girl. . . .'

'Always try and steal my cap-badge, cadets at these little parties,' said Sergeant-Major Dickens. 'So I leave it behind.'

Lilburne nodded.

'So this girl,' went on the drill adjutant, 'marches into the cage and strips off all her clothes and looks at the lions . . .'

Major Hawksworth began a limerick, beating time with his fist. The Emperor Napoleon III had temporarily forgotten the latest crisis from Italy.

'. . . so all the lions, cowed as hell, just came up to her and licked her hands and rubbed their backs against her legs, just like cats.'

A shout of laughter greeted the end of the limerick. Probably all heard it before, thought Lilburne.

'So the manager said, "Why the hell can't you do that?" "So I would," said the chap, "if you'd get rid of all those damned lions." '

'Every cadet at Sandhurst was put back six months and had to do the whole course again,' said Sergeant-Major Dickens.

Lilburne, rather to his surprise, roared with laughter.

Sergeant-Major Dickens charitably put it down to the consumption of spirits. Odd lot of cadets, though, he thought.

The party, headed by Major Hawksworth, his resemblance to Napoleon III increased by his blue uniform and the artificial light, moved in to dinner. Meynell was giggling uncontrollably about some joke that involved Offenbach. Major Hawksworth, noticing this, attributed his behaviour to drink. He was blissfully unaware of the fantasies certain of his cadets, fresh from a good grounding at school in the history of the Second Empire, weaved around him.

The dinner itself proved to be surprisingly good, and not that combination of soup, chicken, and ice-cream which was to become so familiar to those cadets who in later life became involved in public dinners.

There was, too, a great deal of alcohol in evidence, though by now the cadets paid for it on a subscription basis. Noise and—after the toast of the Queen—smoke filled the air. Major Hawksworth made a short, clipped, military speech. Scovington, still technically in command for the day, replied hesitatingly and somewhat confusedly, but did include, having been dared, several references to Napoleon III's mistresses, plus a long, very pointless, and very bad story about a dancer at the *Folies Bergère*. To the mystification of Major Hawksworth and the instructors this brought the house down.

Ransome, taking pity on the Seaforth captain, unsmiling on his right, thought he had better explain. He leant forward. 'You see, sir,' he said, 'we think Major Hawksworth looks like Napoleon III, though without the beard, of course.'

'Ah,' said the captain profoundly. He moved his dessert plate slightly to the right and looked at Ransome. 'Ah yes, I see.'

Eventually chairs were pushed back; the manager, drawn by the sound, hovered anxiously in the background. With his memories of pre-war military dinners he thought of this as the moment of crisis when horseplay and furniture-breaking had to be prevented. Generations change, however, and he was mistaken; led by their officers, the cadets walked, some over-precisely, some clumsily, out to their waiting coach. The officers, save for Captain Tunnicliffe, got into a private car. He joined the cadets in their coach. With a few shouts from the occupants it moved off into the night.

The Clarendon is some way outside Upshott, and the first part of the journey was along narrow hedge-bounded country lanes. Ransome seated in the gangway began to sing. Others joined in. Soon the rural population of Hampshire was being entertained by the appalling words of the 'Ball at Kerrymuir', sung with feeling. The fresh air that streamed through the top half of the windows was beginning to tell. A solitary matron cycling uprightly to her home was nearly unseated by the blasting chorus:

'Oh, five-and-twenty virgins came doon from Inverness,
And when the ball was over there were five-and-twenty less.'

MacNeil, perhaps his Scots blood was inflamed by the appalling travesties of his native accent, began to shout obscenities out of the window at courting couples momentarily transfixed in the headlights.

Captain Tunnicliffe tried vainly to wrest his dress hat from two cadets who were filling it with the contents of a soda-siphon.

The lights of Upshott appeared, the coach slowed down to observe the speed limit. With this cargo it would be madness to defy the police, the driver realized. The singing became muted. Meynell gathered a group of heads together and whispered.

'Get MacNasty,' he shouted suddenly. Four cadets grabbed MacNeil and fell to the floor, arms and legs waving.

'Steady on,' said Tunnicliffe, though not loudly, his sopping hat in one hand.

''Happens to four-letter men, you know,' said Arkwright by his side.

The coach slowed down at some traffic lights. The struggling group on the floor began to straighten out. Meynell pulled himself clear, holding a pair of trousers. Someone opened the sliding door. The coach stopped for a moment on the red light. Red-and-amber.

'Now,' said Meynell.

Officer-Cadet MacNeil, trouserless, went out into the night.

Green. The coach moved on. Captain Tunnicliffe strained his head round and looked back at a lighted street and a diminishing figure that gesticulated briefly and then grabbed protectively at its underpants.

He shrugged his shoulders and began to squeeze more soda-water out of his cap.

12

LILBURNE, Ransome, and Arkwright travelled up to London the next morning in the same carriage.

All three were slightly white in the face and only Ransome smoked. The other two frequently and irritably refused his offered cigarettes.

Ransome puffed nervously away. 'Do you think, Charles, there'll be any trouble about the row in the barrack rooms last night?'

'Shouldn't think so, no real damage done.'

Arkwright laughed. 'What about my hosepipe?'

'That was only in the washbasins, it will all run away.'

'You know,' said Arkwright, 'I couldn't understand it, when I was holding all you chaps at bay, why Parker kept thrusting himself forward and getting soaked.'

'Especially when he was wearing pyjamas.'

'How long did it take you, Peter, to realize they were your own, that he had gone and put them on?'

'Too late, I'm afraid, Charles.'

'You know, I think Parker's improved tremendously,' said Ransome. 'He tells me he saw the most tremendous session in a car when he was on the exercise. Right under his nose.'

'What do you mean, George? That that makes him a good chap?'

'No, no, Charles, he couldn't move.'

'I don't doubt that.'

Ransome caught the eye of the elderly lady in the farther corner and dropped the subject.

'What worries me slightly,' said Lilburne, 'is my prize black with the fire-extinguisher. You see, I saw a peaked cap in the corridor and thought it was old Scovington trying to assert his authority at the last minute. So I let him have it. Of course it was Miller, the provost sergeant. Wonder if he recognized me?'

'Shouldn't think so. Hardly in a state to see anything. Christ, he was livid.' Arkwright smiled reminiscently. 'His uniform was ruined.'

'Best thing of the night, I thought,' said Ransome, 'was Mac-Nasty in his underpants in the street.' Privately he was relieved that he hadn't been the victim himself.

'My God, yes!'

'Splendid effort, that.'

They sat back and thought about MacNeil without his trousers, impervious to the astonished looks of the elderly lady.

It was only at Waterloo that she could contain her curiosity no longer. She looked surprised when Arkwright and Lilburne helped her lift her bags from the rack.

'Tell me,' she said, 'what are those white things on your lapels for?'

'Penal battalion, madam,'said Lilburne, gravely, hanging his head.

The elderly lady looked at the locks of her cases and left swiftly.

Arkwright moved off through the barrier to catch a connection, Lilburne and Ransome followed more leisurely.

'About the party tonight,' said Ransome. Lilburne's heart sank a little. 'Where shall we meet, Charles?'

'Well, I'm coming from South Ken, you're in Hampstead already. Shall we meet somewhere and have a drink first?'

'Yes, let's do that. I know a splendid pub called the Vine, near the Heath. Shall we meet there at seven?'

'Say seven-thirty for safety. How do I find it?'

Ransome sketched a few roads on the back of a piece of paper. 'If in doubt,' he said, 'ask a policeman.'

Lilburne put the paper in his pocket. 'What time is the party, anyway?'

'Eightish, nineish, doesn't really matter. Given by a girl called Naomi Janowitz.'

'How much?'

Ransome frowned at him and pronounced it carefully. 'Her old man's away, simply vast house. Terribly wealthy.'

Lilburne wondered why not 'rich', remembered his Nancy Mitford, and kept silent.

'It'll go on all night, Charles, but if you're bored you can always creep away.'

'I shan't be, George.'

'Are you bringing your car?'

'Don't think it's worth it. Anyhow, see what I feel like.'

'Right, Charles,' said Ransome unnecessarily. 'Seven-thirty, the Vine, see you there.'

Lilburne smiled and half stood to attention.

'Wilco.'

They moved away from each other in the crowd, Ransome towards the Underground, Lilburne not knowing quite what he intended, save to leave Ransome.

'Charles.' Lilburne turned. Ransome was waving his hand. 'Charles, bring a bottle. Something cheap.'

Lilburne waved back in acknowledgement and walked towards the street with the crowd. Having made a quick calculation he realized that the price of the cheapest nastiest bottle of wine prevented the luxury of a taxi home. If his father was using the car he would probably have to walk to Hampstead.

By five o'clock in the evening, however, Lilburne felt better disposed to the world generally and Ransome's, or rather this girl Janowitz's, party in particular.

He was sitting alone in his father's Kensington flat. He had spent a long time in his bath, and was now wondering how long he could lie back in a chair and look at the few London trees outside before he started to change.

His father earlier in the day had been in one of his rare, benevolent, men-of-the-world moods. He had treated Charles to an excellent lunch and had insisted on giving him a five-pound note, muttering something about Army pay being disgraceful. Charles had mentioned his thirty shillings per week perhaps a little obviously, but the enforced expenditure on a bottle rankled, and he thought justified such obvious tactics.

His father's mood was such that Charles had found no difficulty, after referring to the favourable report he had received, in getting permission to borrow the car for the evening.

'Hampstead, a party,' said his father; 'will you enjoy yourself?'

'I don't really know,' said Charles.

'No, I suppose not. Anyway, be careful with the car. You'll find that the clutch is a bit odd in second.' The car was a 1938 Bentley sports saloon, his father's prize possession, and kept in perfect order.

His father branched out on a diatribe on the iniquities of garages and garage mechanics, one of his favourite subjects. Charles had listened dutifully.

Now, his father had left him at tea-time, for an unspecified appointment. Charles luxuriated alone.

He forced himself out of the chair, found a long-playing record of Beethoven's *Eroica*, put it on the turntable of the radio-gram, and went into his bedroom to change, leaving the door open.

He changed into a dark-grey suit and put on his school tie, decided that was wrong for Hampstead, and tried a light-blue and white-spotted creation his father had once brought him from Italy. Looking at himself in the mirror he thought that with the very short military haircut, almost *en brosse*, the tie was a mistake. He brushed his hair down again in a vain attempt to make it look longer and returned to the sober stripes of the old school tie. To hell with Hampstead, he thought.

Next door Beethoven's hero had died. The funeral games had been played round the pyre and the French horn was echoing past deeds of grandeur, muted and hollow.

Lilburne filled his cigarette-case from a box of his father's. A birthday present of his mother's, he remembered.

The staccato third movement began; Lilburne listened, beating time with his free hand as he moved around the flat collecting his personal belongings, a penknife, his wallet, and some keys.

He held the car keys in his hand for a moment and looked down out of the window at the gleaming black bonnet. With a sense of proud possession he turned off the radiogram and walked out of the front door to the car in his best casual manner. He was rather pleased with himself. If his mother had seen him at that moment she would have recognized his father at what she called 'his worst'.

After a pleasant but hectic drive through London—he drove carelessly and always too fast—Lilburne found the Vine at the top of a steep hill. The climb had not done the gearbox much good, but as if to banish his father's imagined admonitions he drew up to the forecourt with a flourish and a minor cascade of gravel.

Inside the sparsely populated bar he saw Ransome almost immediately, standing awkwardly by a table-lamp in a bottle set on the bar.

'Hello, Charles.'

'Hello, George, took a hell of a time getting here, sorry.'

They looked at each other. It was the first time they had seen each other in civilian clothes. Ransome took in Lilburne's tie, his expensive suit with its narrow trousers, and his well-made suède shoes. Lilburne noticed Ransome's sand-coloured sports coat and grey flannels, and the fact that he was wearing army-issue brown shoes.

'You shouldn't have dressed up, Charles, it's not that sort

of party. Rather the reverse.' Ransome's eyes closed conspiratorily at this witticism.

'All I'd got,' said Lilburne, embarrassed. 'Let's have a drink, and what about a sandwich? I'm going to have a couple of those.' He pointed at a plastic case.

Ransome accepted the drink.

Conversation inevitably turned to Ypres, though the easy communion when both had been cloaked in khaki anonymity seemed to have disappeared. Lilburne ate his sandwiches and drank sparingly, almost as a protest to Ransome who seemed to be intent on getting drunk before he even got to the party.

At half past eight Lilburne looked meaningly at his watch. 'I suppose, George, we ought to . . .'

'All right,' said Ransome, almost reluctantly. He reached behind a chair for a brown-paper-covered bottle. 'Hock,' he said, 'what have you brought?'

'Oh, my God! I've completely forgotten. I wonder if I can get something here. Would half a bottle of whisky do?'

'Always welcome, old man.'

Lilburne bought his whisky, put the flat bottle into his pocket, and they went out to the car.

'Lovely job,' said Ransome, patting a wing with a moist hand.

Lilburne put on his most unconcerned expression as they drove off. He made a mental note to wipe that wing before he returned the car to his father.

The 'simply vast house' turned out to be a moderate-sized white neo-Georgian building looking out over Hampstead Heath and approached by a semi-circular drive. Lilburne parked his car in the road, between a small battered M.G. and a converted legend-adorned taxi.

Ransome rang the bell and at the same time pushed open the door. The inside of the house did indeed spell wealth, thought Lilburne. Recently acquired, said his father's voice. He stared at two men in sweaters sitting on the stairs. They stared back. The noise of a gramophone playing calypsos came through an open door. 'In here,' said Ransome. Lilburne followed him.

Twenty or thirty people almost filled a pleasantly proportioned room looking out on to a lawn. Nearly all the women seemed to be dressed in black and the men in bright sweaters.

A tall thin girl with a peaked shiny face came towards them.

'Hello, Naomi,' said Ransome. 'This is Charles Lilburne.'

'Charles, I can remember that. I'm Naomi.'

'How do you do,' said Charles.

Two blue eyes took in his formal suit.

'I hear you're having the most awful time with military sadists.'

'Well . . .'

'We've got some drink,' said Ransome. 'Charles has brought whisky.'

'Oh, lovely. I'll take them into the kitchen. That adorable bearded man from the Slade is mixing punch.'

Lilburne smiled weakly. She took the bottles, disappeared, and came back a minute later with two glasses of a pale-yellow liquid.

'You know everybody, George. Make Charles at home.' Another glance at Lilburne's suit and she moved towards the small crowd round the gramophone.

Lilburne took a sip from his glass and reached for his cigarette-case.

'Nice girl, Naomi,' said Ransome. Lilburne nodded through his cigarette smoke.

'Chap I know,' said Ransome. He started to push his way through the press. A tall thin young man with black hair brushed straight back waved to him.

Lilburne rested his arm on a sideboard and looked around. Conversation and calypso fought for dominance.

'Oh, I never have bin, educated at Lincoln's Inn,' howled the gramophone, rather surprisingly.

A small blonde girl stood in front of Lilburne. 'They're all originals,' she said. 'Naomi's brother, the proper one, brought them back from Jamaica.'

'I'll not go back to the Caribbee, I want to appear at the Old Bailee,' yelled the machine.

'I think the rhythm's terribly sexy, don't you?'

'Fearfully,' said Lilburne. 'Do you smoke?'

Someone turned the gramophone up. More people began to come in at the door. The small blonde girl began to shout. Lilburne, impelled by politeness, moved with her into the thick of the crowd.

'What do you do?' yelled the small blonde girl.

Lilburne began to shout back. A man with an Assyrian beard filled their glasses to overflowing from a large china water-jug. He looked at Lilburne's tie. 'I was at Eton,' he said.

'I'm sorry,' said Lilburne, mopping his cuff with his handkerchief.

The small blonde girl introduced in dumb show a small blond man who looked like a pig. He bared his teeth at Lilburne and put his arm round the girl. She disengaged the arm and continued to shout. Lilburne stretched to his full height so as not to hear her and produced a cigarette-holder. He found that by nodding his head and puffing at his cigarette alternately he could keep up his end in the conversation.

'Well, my dear. The thing was finished, so finished it just wasn't true.' A female voice.

'I know so well.' A near-male voice. Lilburne tried to turn his head to find the owner.

In the corner a girl began to remove her black sweater. Disappointingly, she had another one underneath. Lilburne lowered his head to his drink.

What sounded like a banging of drums and the gramophone stopped abruptly.

'More music, for God's sake, otherwise Peter'll play his guitar.'

Conversation became audible.

'Well, that's stopped. So this appalling military person said he always went to horse-shows, so what could I say?'

'And the novel ends with a really tremendous twist, but I won't tell you. Anyway, you've probably guessed.'

'They've all been dead for years.'

'You have guessed.'

'We never see him now. Sheila says he's very happy at the House and marches about in tweed suits.'

'I've met the new one. He's at least fifty but he has got this daily column so I suppose that helps.'

Lilburne saw Ransome's red face moving towards him. He pushed his glass in front of him and went to join him.

'Ah,' said Ransome, 'enjoying yourself? Damned hot, isn't it?' He wiped his brow.

Lilburne's eye caught the face of a tall girl talking to a man of about thirty by the french windows. 'Who's that, George?'

'That's Jo Mason, splendid girl, not your type, I'm afraid.'

'She's got a frightfully good figure.'

'I know, had an affair with her once. Passionate as hell. Insists on wearing black stockings.'

'Well, she's not now.'

'No, I mean when . . .'

'I should like to meet her.'

Ransome shrugged his shoulders. 'Not your type, though,' he said.

Ransome elbowed his way towards the windows. Lilburne with an effort downed the contents of his glass, put it on a bookshelf, and followed him.

He found himself looking over Ransome's shoulder at a girl some years older than himself and a good bit taller.

Apparently introductions had been made in his absence.

'Terrible party, isn't it?' she said.

'Yes, I wish I wasn't wearing this suit.'

'You're in the Army with George?' said the man.

'Yes.'

'Enjoy it? I hated my time.'

'*Servitudes et grandeurs militaires.* More servitude at present, though we are promised a band.'

Jo Mason laughed. 'The drink's terrible,' she said, 'but I would like another.'

'I'll get you one. We can have it in the garden.'

'Fast worker,' said Ransome.

Lilburne ignored him. He had taken the plunge. He bowed. 'Perhaps, madam, you would care for a turn round the garden?' he said. 'I'll be back.' He took her glass and walked towards the door.

'I like your friend Charles,' said Jo.

'Not your type,' said Ransome.

'What do you mean by that?' said the man.

Lilburne appeared with two filled glasses, he stood back to allow Jo to precede him into the garden. As she walked through the french windows Lilburne caught the eye of the man with Ransome. Perhaps he didn't like the party either.

Lilburne and Jo strolled over the turf. He looked at her covertly. She had a nose more aquiline than Grecian and there were shadows under her eyes. He wondered how old she was.

He looked at her hand holding a glass. Large for a woman but strong, not the 'little fat hands' his mother said were the sign of a mean nature.

They sat down on a wooden garden-seat and looked back at the house. Lights were being switched on, the music had moved eastwards to Europe, and a woman's voice rose and fell rhythmically.

'Flamenco, isn't it?' said Jo.

'No, fado, Portuguese, no clapping,' said Charles.

Afterwards Lilburne could remember little of the details of what they talked about. He remembered going into the house and finding his bottle of whisky half consumed. He took it out into the garden with him.

As he walked towards Jo, now hardly discernible in the shadows, he wondered whether he was being sincere. Was his conversation about music and art just a 'line' or not? He enjoyed talking to this girl, certainly, but was he putting forward his ideas about life and listening to hers entirely uninfluenced by her physical attraction? Anyhow, what about her, was she sincere? Perhaps she was bored stiff, perhaps . . . Oh, he didn't know.

He sat down beside her and poured out two measures of whisky.

He began to talk quite seriously about the Army. The fado still balanced on quavering half-tones telling its story of sad blighted loves.

Lilburne stopped in mid sentence and looked at Jo. She stared unwinking back at him. He knew enough to know that he was expected to kiss her. 'Somehow,' he said, 'I feel terribly sad, that voice and the garden and even the Army.' He leaned forward and kissed her.

The tip of her tongue ran round inside his mouth, probing and tantalizing. He began to move his hand up the middle of her back. She seemed to have nothing on under her sweater.

'Jo.' A shout; a suited figure stood silhouetted against the light from the french windows.

'Oh, Charles, it's Peter, you know, he was with me. He brought me here in his car.'

'Jo—I'm going, do you want a lift home?'

Lilburne squeezed her hand. 'I've got a car,' he said, 'if that worries you.'

'No, thanks, Peter, good night.' Jo raised her voice.

'Well, good night.' Peter did not sound pleased. The figure moved out of the light.

'Oh dear,' said Lilburne, 'I felt sorry for him.'

'Hypocrite and liar,' said Jo, pushing her breast against his shirt-front. Lilburne smiled and dropped his hand to her knee.

The music from the gramophone stopped and some time later the french windows opened. A streak of light lanced across the grass. A man and a woman, their arms round each other, walked undecidedly across the lawn.

'Competition,' whispered Lilburne in Jo's ear.

She patted at her skirt. 'Let's go inside,' she said. They stood up.

Lilburne addressed himself to the other couple. 'Would you care for a seat?' he said.

They laughed.

Inside the drawing-room the overhead lights had been switched off. Table-lamps burned, casting light and small shadows over couples lying in corners and with their backs against the wall. One solitary young man in a light-blue pullover cradled a guitar in his lap. He looked asleep.

Charles followed Jo as she made her way into the kitchen.

Naomi Janowitz was cutting a long French loaf into sections. The little blond man who looked like a pig was pouring coffee into an assortment of cups and mugs.

'Jo, darling,' said Naomi, 'I thought you left with Peter.' She noticed Lilburne. 'Oh,' she said, 'would you like some coffee and something to eat?'

'Thank you,' said Lilburne, and took two cups from the little blond man.

Naomi picked up a tray. 'Must feed the starving masses,' she said to no one in particular. The little blond man held back the door for her. He winked at Lilburne and followed her out.

Lilburne watched Jo eating a large piece of roll stuffed with cheese and lettuce.

'You've got lipstick on your shirt,' she said, between mouthfuls.

'Don't care,' said Lilburne. He found difficulty in adjusting his mind to the prosaic business of coffee and sandwiches in the kitchen. He put his cup down. 'I think you're terribly——' he began.

Jo put her finger to her lips. 'Not in the kitchen,' she said. She took his hand and led him out of the door and along the hall.

Sprawled on the stairs was Ransome, breathing heavily. His face was very white.

Jo stepped out of her shoes and began to tiptoe up the stairs past him. He opened his eyes and looked up.

'Lovely, lovely legs,' he said drunkenly.

Lilburne, following, avoided an outstretched hand.

'Oh no,' said Ransome loudly. 'Officer-Cadet Lilburne, take his name, 'orrible man.'

'Oh, shut up, George,' said Lilburne. Jo had reached the top of the stairs. He bent down swiftly. 'Not on parade for a bit, old chap,' he whispered.

Ransome lifted an unwilling hand in salute. 'Naked but not idle,' he murmured. Lilburne looked down at him for a moment and stepped quickly up the remaining stairs.

Jo had opened a door. He followed her into a room. The moonlight half illuminated what was obviously the Janowitz parents' bedroom.

'There's a catch on the door, Charles.' Lilburne automatically clicked it home. Jo stood for a moment by the window. Lilburne sank his mouth into the hair at the back of her neck. He began with a quite false air of confidence to remove her sweater. She wriggled out of it, he cupped his hands under her breasts. 'What about the gang downstairs?' he whispered.

'Darling,' she said, 'what a cautious soldier. It's all right,' she said, 'Naomi's a curious, sex-starved bitch but she's an old friend.'

Lilburne's eye caught a silver-framed photograph of the Janowitz elders looking steadfastly to their front. He stretched out a hand and laid it flat on its face.

Jo laughed. Suddenly she sat down on the bed and began to remove her stockings. Lilburne knelt down beside her and kissed her bared thighs. He had seen quite a few French films after leaving school.

13

THE Commandant, the drill adjutant, and R.S.M. Muxlow all pulled at Officer-Cadet Lilburne's shoulder-straps—he woke up. Jo, already dressed, smiled at him. 'I thought, Charles, you'd be doing P.T. by an open window or something.'

Lilburne shuddered.

The ghost of Kathleen Ferrier sang in rounded phrases from below, 'What is life without you?'

'That will be Naomi,' said Jo, 'she's mad about that record. If we're lucky she'll give us some coffee.'

Lilburne looked at his watch and rubbed his chin. 'No razor,' he said.

The record still asked its rhetorical question.

'Sorry, Jo.' Lilburne shook his head. 'Be alive in a moment.'

'I'll go down while you surface,' she said and disappeared round the door.

Lilburne forced himself into his clothes. His formal suit felt stiff and uncomfortable. His collar grated on his neck. He found a bathroom, and trying not to look at a decaying glass of gin-and-orange left on a shelf and a cigarette burnt out in the bath, borrowed a toothbrush and a monogrammed Janowitz hairbrush.

A Handelian organ concerto took the place of Kathleen Ferrier, its theme seemed to be a decorative version of 'Bobby Shafto'.

Lilburne tiptoed downstairs. He wondered who had removed Ransome.

Naomi Janowitz sat on a stool in the kitchen. She looked as if she had been there all night. The small man who looked like a pig, and whose fate it seemed to be to remain permanently unintroduced, smirked at her side. Perhaps after all, thought Lilburne, she had not been there all night.

'Ah,' said the little blond man.

'Ah,' said Lilburne, and inclined his head towards Naomi.

'Here's some coffee,' said Jo. She handed him a mug. 'When you've drunk it you must take me away to buy some cigarettes.'

'I've got some, I think.' Jo silenced him with a look. 'No, I haven't,' went on Lilburne, who believed in keeping up appearances. He solemnly patted his pockets and then for the benefit of the company shook his head. Naomi and the small blond man looked at him as if he were an idiot.

Lilburne drank his coffee almost at a gulp. He hesitated to look at Jo directly, as he still saw her body beneath her clothes.

'We must go,' he said, addressing the kitchen sink.

'Lovely party, thanks so much,' said Jo.

'Yes,' said Lilburne, 'thank you.'

' 'Bye,' said Naomi, she waved a hand.

Lilburne's arm jerked in a barrack-square reflex into a half-salute. He caught the eye of the small blond man, and said, 'Good-bye, Henry.'

'My name's not . . .' said the small blond man, automatically, but Jo and Lilburne were already in the hall. It still retained an air of wealth, but had acquired some subtle undertone of the battle-field. Handel, if it was Handel, thumped away cheerfully until the door shut.

In the car Lilburne offered Jo his cigarette-case. 'What was the matter with those two?' he said.

'Best bedroom taken over, I suppose, or else they didn't hit it off in some way. He probably didn't fall madly for Naomi.'

'I thought he was queer.'

'Did you? By the way, why did you call him Henry?'

'I once had a small rubber pig called Henry, it looked very like him.'

Jo half smiled. 'Naomi was furious, but she'll be ringing me up within a week. She's mad to get into the art world—why, heaven knows.'

Lilburne's eyes asked a question.

'I'm a commercial artist, you know, madly gay illustrations of detergents and tins of coffee.'

'You must draw me a tin of metal-polish as a present for our sergeant-major.'

Jo stared uncomprehendingly.

'Joke,' said Lilburne; he pressed the starter.

Lilburne drove carelessly down towards Kensington. Hampstead with its mixture of rural and sordid was soon left behind. The wider streets of Central London, what Lilburne thought of as really London, stretched around them. On a Sunday morning, with the sun shining, the open spaces filled in with blue sky assumed an air of Canaletto. Londoners trying to look Italianate wore sun-glasses, pointed their toes, and walked gracefully in the light.

Lilburne began to hum the air from *Eurydice*.

'You know,' he said, 'I used to think if you had a Bentley you automatically got a pretty girl to go with it.' He looked at Jo. 'I was right.'

She smiled.

'Right, and then left,' she said.

Lilburne turned a corner and parked flashily with too much squealing of tyres by the entrance to a mews. 'I feel very happy,' he said. 'May I give you a ring when I get back from Buckinghamshire?'

'Yes, of course, Charles, but don't be disappointed if I'm not in. My job takes me all over the place. Kensington 3970.'

Lilburne leaned over her, pushed open the door. He experienced a faint thrill of sensuality at the sight of her knees as she got out of the car.

He watched her walk down the cobbles of the mews.

His hand hovered over the horn to call her back. She let herself into a doorway and disappeared.

He turned the car. In the centre of a square a middle-aged man in a beret was playing an accordion. Lilburne drove back to his father's flat. It really was a splendid day, he decided.

His father looked up from his late breakfast. 'Ah, Charles,' he said, 'a person called Ransome rang up. I've written his number down. I told him I didn't know when you'd be back. Is the car all right? I thought it sounded a bit rough as you drove up.'

By Tuesday Lilburne was almost reconciled to his visit to the Churchouses. His mind went back to the party in Hampstead but he kept on telling himself that this was purely luck. His leave had been planned on the basis that he should spend two or three days with Nick's parents. He had been invited and had accepted. There was nothing he could do about it now. Anyhow, he had rung Jo's number on Monday, twice, and there had been no reply.

He tried again before leaving for the station to catch his train to Aylesbury, but again there was no answer.

Churchouse was waiting at Aylesbury station, sitting in the family saloon. He was wearing cavalry twill trousers and a checked open-necked shirt. His fair hair looked as if it had been bleached in the sun.

'Hallo, Charles,' he said, 'throw your kit in the back. We're supposed to be home for lunch.'

Lilburne got in beside him.

'By the way, Charles, how was your party with Ransome?'

'Odd,' said Lilburne, and told him. Churchouse nodded seriously as he drove carefully along the white-gravelled Buckinghamshire by-roads. He made no comment on Lilburne's behaviour, merely saying at the end of the recital, 'Curious fellow, Ransome, I wonder how he'll get on in his regiment.'

Lilburne thought the observation could equally well apply to himself, but he couldn't make up his mind whether Churchouse believed his own personal account or not.

The Churchouse home proved to be what estate agents, contrary to their usual habit of verbal magnification, call a cottage. It was in fact a long low sizable house, and its only resemblance to an agricultural dwelling was that it was painted white.

Churchouse drove down a winding made-up path to a side door shaded by small artificial-looking trees.

A tall grey-haired woman in a tweed suit emerged. 'You're Charles,' she said, adding rather disconcertingly, 'How very different people look from what you imagine.'

'I'm sorry,' said Charles; he smiled and took her outstretched hand. He was relieved to find that she at least was English.

'Nicky will bring in your bag. Come and meet my husband.'

Lilburne obediently followed her through a modern kitchen and into a long drawing-room which seemed to be filled with eighteenth-century furniture and silver-framed photographs. He shook hands with Churchouse's father. The family resemblance was strong. Professor—or was it Doctor?—Churchouse was over six foot, with thinning fair hair and his son's immobile face. His voice when he spoke revealed little of a German accent. His phrasing however was more precise than that of a native Englishman. His clothes were tweedy and rather untidy. Lilburne, who had rather feared a shaven-headed, booted Prussian was again relieved. He accepted an extraordinarily strong gin-and-tonic gratefully.

Lunch, which was served on Nick's arrival, went smoothly enough. The two boys told the familiar military anecdotes, successfully adapting the coarser military expressions to polite usage, and the two parents appeared to be amused. Churchouse senior revealed a mordant sense of humour, but appeared to be careful not to poke too much fun at the British Army, probably for fear of offending Lilburne.

Mrs. Churchouse chatted gaily on throughout the meal, making fun of her husband's scientific interests and her son's military ambitions. She laid her hand on Lilburne's. 'You've no idea what it's like to live in a house with two Junkers like these,' she said. Lilburne felt slightly embarrassed, but the two male Churchouses both laughed. It was obviously a family joke.

Lilburne, looking at Dr. Churchouse and his wife, contrasted them favourably with his own parents, egocentrically leading their separate, pointless lives. He wanted to know more about his host, this rather quiet man now sipping his coffee and smoking a cigarette. He wanted to fill in the gaps; he knew from Nick that his father had been a subaltern in the 1st Uhlans of the Guard in the Kaiser's war, and that he had for a time in the twenties lived in Poland and then that he came to England as a political refugee after Hitler assumed power in 1933. Lilburne wanted to know the details of this interesting career, in fact he wanted Dr. Churchouse to do the forbidden thing, to embark on a monologue beginning, 'I remember when I was a young man.'

Emboldened perhaps by the hock he had been drinking—the Churchouses seemed to be good hosts, he reflected—Lilburne leaned forward. 'I suppose in the old German Army, sir . . .'

'Oh, very different, Charles, very different. I remember, oh, it must have been before 1914 on the autumn manœuvres . . .' He paused. 'But then my wife says I am not to bore people with my military reminiscences.' He smiled in the same sad wintry manner his son had inherited. 'We shall have a talk later.' He began to shift his chair back from the table.

'Nicky,' he said, 'will you try and shoot that jay for me this afternoon?'

'Charles and I will try our best strategy and tactics.'

Lilburne admitted defeat, drank the remains of his coffee, and after changing in the pleasant bedroom he had been allotted joined Nick who was fitting a 12-bore together.

'Charles, we have a curious selection of weapons in this house. I can offer you this or a .22 or a very light 4.10 I used to have as a boy.'

'I'll take the 12-bore,' said Lilburne, 'and leave you with the .22. You're probably a more accurate shot than I am.' He took the gun and put half a dozen cartridges in his pocket.

They placed themselves under cover at opposite ends of the vegetable garden, the most recent site of the jay's depredations, and waited.

Lilburne fitted two cartridges into the breech and made himself comfortable. He rested his gun in his lap and lit a cigarette.

The blue sky shimmered through the trees above his head. The smoke from his cigarette spiralled straight upwards. After his excellent lunch he felt comfortably replete. Jay or no jay it was a pleasant way to spend an afternoon. He looked at the pattern of the leaves around him. A small bird chirped in the undergrowth. The world was very peaceful. His thoughts wandered to Jo Mason. What had she said to him during one of the pauses in their hectic love-making? 'You have a splendid cynical pose, Charles, but you'll grow up.' Why should she say that? Of course she had known she was the first woman he had slept with, but why this assumption of superior knowledge? Was he such an obvious poseur? Anyhow, why shouldn't he be cynical? A blackbird's alarm note repeated to his front. He sensed rather than heard a bird alight in the tree over his head. He swivelled round on the shooting-stick, raising his gun cautiously; the tip of a black balancing tail, a glimpse of a pinkish-brown head swiftly withdrawn. Lilburne eased the safety-catch. Dare he risk a shot at the head? The blackbird cried harshly again, a swoop, and the jay was on another branch more to his right but farther away. Choke, thought Lilburne, at that distance. Its tail jerked, its wings opened for an instant to steady itself. Lilburne lifted his gun, felt the shooting-stick overbalancing, and pulled the left trigger. The explosion echoed, small birds chattered, the jay's wings drooped, and it flopped clumsily head first to the ground. Lilburne stood up, caught the shooting-stick, and walked over to where the bird had fallen. It lay on its side, one blue-edged wing extended, a beady eye winked and faded, a pulse stopped in its throat. Lilburne prodded it with the shooting-stick. A little over twelve inches of pink and brilliant blue-and-black feathers, an eater of eggs, and a mimic, full of guile and curiosity, was dead.

Lilburne shoved at its chest with his foot; his thoughts had gone to Tunnicliffe's story of his battery commander killed in the Normandy orchard.

Churchouse ran up. 'Get him, Charles?'

'Oh yes,' said Lilburne casually. 'Handsome birds, aren't they?' He broke his gun and unloaded.

Churchouse picked up the jay; its head flopped backwards, and its beak opened. 'I'll hang it up in the vegetable garden to keep the others off,' he said.

'All you'll get,' said Lilburne, 'is lots of small birds coming to tear feathers out of their old enemy. I can't stand the sight of gamekeepers' gallows, anyway.'

'Well, you shot it, Charles,' said Churchouse.

They walked slowly back to the house. The heat was becoming oppressive, overhead the sky was opaque, the air was very still, and the twittering of small birds became shrill.

'Thunder very soon,' said Churchouse. Lilburne nodded; he really wished he hadn't shot the jay.

That night after dinner Mrs. Churchouse produced an old Bruno Walter recording of Beethoven's Ninth Symphony, and as the thunder rolled round in the distance they sat back and listened, sipped at glasses of whisky, and pursued their own private thoughts. Later Lilburne, the first to retire that night, lay back in bed with only a sheet over him, and enjoyed hearing the swish of the long-delayed rain.

He thought about life, and snatches of Beethoven themes

would go through his head. He wondered about the jay and Jo Mason. Heightened by the drama of the thunder and the rain, it all seemed highly significant.

He turned over and burrowed with his head at the pillow. Reluctantly he decided he couldn't listen to the rain all night. He wondered if Churchouse was still awake. Did everyone become introspective living idly in the country? What was his mother's phrase? 'Buried in the country.' Hardly applicable, he felt, and closed his eyes.

A gutter gurgled by his window and the rain still poured down.

The rest of Lilburne's stay meandered gently. The Churchouses were good but not demanding hosts. Lilburne ate and drank too much, but justified it all on the grounds of the hard life to come when he returned to Ypres.

Lilburne liked the whole Churchouse family. They seemed to be sensible and confident about life. It was obviously important that Nick—Lilburne had not failed to notice the use of the more foreign-sounding Nicky at home—should be commissioned, and so, as it were, be accepted in the English social scene. Equally, of course, it was to be expected of any male Churchouse that he should have some minor success in the profession of arms that the family had followed for so many generations.

For the rest, the Churchouses seemed to possess a serenity all their own.

Lilburne wondered if in the case of Dr. Churchouse this was an attitude of mind he had been led to adopt, having seen so much of human chance and change and misfortune.

Left alone with him on Wednesday night, Lilburne had tried vainly to draw him out on this subject.

Dr. Churchouse had admittedly talked about the past, but with no rancour or indeed any false romanticism.

He had shown Lilburne an album of photographs when he realized he was interested and had some knowledge of Germany before the 1914–18 war.

Yet he had said little and certainly nothing of the 'good old days' as they looked together at pictures of military groups and parades. Many of the young men in high stiff collars and archaic peaked caps must have been colleagues and friends, but there was no over-sentimentalized reaction to portraits that must have aroused memories and recollections. Simply entered in white ink under many was some such comment as: 'Killed Somme.' There was a large sepia-tinted photograph of the Churchouse grandfather in his full-dress uniform of a general, his chest covered in medals, and a hard face staring belligerently out at the world from under a spiked helmet.

'He was a bit of an old devil, my father,' said Dr. Churchouse.

When they came to another full-length portrait, this time of a young *unter-leutnant*, his left hand resting on an enormous cavalry sabre, and his right awkwardly holding a plumed helmet in the traditional military pose of the time, Dr. Churchouse laughed. Underneath was written: 'Myself, when very young, 1913.'

'That was the day I was commissioned. The Kaiser inspected us and my mother and sister were very proud, but I was just uncomfortable. I had a boil on my neck under my collar, so perhaps I looked even more Prussian than usual. Certainly I couldn't move my head even if I'd wanted to.'

Lilburne smiled and turned the pages. The gold lace and the epaulettes disappeared, the occasional glimpse of the Kaiser or the Crown Prince did not recur. He came to photographs in bad light of field-grey figures set against backgrounds of picket lines or shelled French farmhouses.

Three officers, leaning their backs against a limber. Underneath: 'Carl, Myself, and the Adjutant, Festubert, 1916.'

'Carl was my brother; he was killed about a week later,' said Dr. Churchouse.

'Festubert,' said Lilburne, 'an uncle of mine was there.' He stopped, both of them realized the implication.

Dr. Churchouse got up. 'Well,' he said, 'I'll leave you with the album. I have a hard day tomorrow. Good night, Charles.'

'Good night, sir.'

Lilburne continued to turn over the pages. The other side of the picture, he thought. How many times had he seen similar, but khaki-coloured, groups in the homes of his relations?

He turned back to the pre-1914 era. 'Crown Prince Wilhelm inspects squadrons before the Autumn Manœuvres', he read. He heard Dr. Churchouse moving upstairs. Lilburne was still slightly surprised and intrigued that this quiet man had seen so much history. Yet it was Lilburne not Dr. Churchouse who tended to romanticize it. He suspected that Mrs. Churchouse had probably instructed and persuaded her husband that talking about his German past was emotional and of course un-English.

On Thursday Lilburne received a telephone call from his father, who wanted to know if he was coming back to London or proceeding straight to Aldershot on Friday.

The rather petulant voice sounded as if it issued from a tin box.

'Your mother rang me, Charles; wanted to know where you were, what you were doing. Couldn't tell her, so I suppose you'll be hearing from her.'

Lilburne received this information and went on to tell his father that he intended to stay with the Churchouses until Friday when they would give him a lift to Aldershot.

'Good, good,' said the sharp voice. 'Tell me, Charles, this new part of your O.C.T.U. Will you get days off and things?'

'Oh, I think we get a bit more spare time, rather more civilized, you know.'

'That's what I thought, excellent.'

Lilburne could not see why this should please his father particularly but he did not enquire.

'Ah, well, I must ring off, but one thing, Charles: I found a rather nasty cheap lipstick in the car the other day, and there's a dent on the left wing.'

Lilburne smiled to himself. 'Well, Father, the lipstick I am responsible for, but not the dent.'

'Ah yes, what shall I do with it?'

'Throw it away.'

'What?'

'The lipstick, I should keep the car,' said Lilburne slowly.

His father's metallic laugh did not sound really amused. The voice became more distant.

'By the way, Charles, there's a letter here. I opened it. Says you have a place at St. Mark's after your service.'

'Oh, splendid,' said Lilburne; the whole thing seemed as remote as his father's voice.

'Better write and tell your mother, she'll be pleased.'

Wasn't *he*?

'Good-bye, Charles.'

'Good-bye, Father.' Lilburne put down the receiver. Churchouse had entered the room during the latter part of the conversation.

'My father, Nick,' said Lilburne. He shrugged his shoulders. 'He's quite mad.'

Churchouse smiled politely, as if accepting the picture of Lilburne senior confined in a strait jacket using his telephone from a padded cell.

On Thursday evening the Churchouses invited half a dozen people in for cocktails, among them was a very military brigadier whose tailor had obviously taken a dislike to him. Lilburne found himself talking to the brigadier's daughter, a solid butter-coloured girl who planted both her feet firmly on the ground in the regulation 'at ease' position and addressed him on the subject of a friend of hers who painted horses.

Lilburne mumbled something about 'What colour?' but his heart wasn't in it. The brigadier was doubtless useful to the Churchouses, or rather to their son, and the rest of the guests were so tweedy that Lilburne wondered if the invitation had said at the bottom: 'Fancy Dress. Come as an Englishman.'

Why he wanted the Churchouses not to be so thoroughly English Lilburne couldn't really work out. Perhaps he was disappointed, perhaps it was just that his pleasant stay was now accelerating rapidly to its end. Now he was used to the house and the feel of his bed and the view from the windows he had to move on. He decided he must be a very static creature.

He left the Brigadier's daughter in the middle of a description of a pony-show and on impulse went to Dr. Churchouse's study and put through a call to Jo Mason's number. He had a vague idea of rushing to London on Friday and seeing her.

After a time a female voice answered.

'Jo,' said Lilburne.

'I'm sorry, Jo's away for a week in Birmingham. I am Naomi Janowitz. I'm looking after her flat. Can I give her a message?'

'No, thank you,' said Lilburne, dropping his voice. 'Just tell her Stanley Baldwin called.'

'Stanley Baldwin, certainly.'

'Good-bye and thank you, Miss Janowitz,' said Lilburne, replacing the receiver.

He rejoined the party in the drawing-room. He took a large gin from Nick Churchouse and stood on the edge of a group listening to the Brigadier, who was telling a funny story about a brigadier.

After tea on Friday Mrs. Churchouse volunteered to drive Charles and Nick back to Upshott.

As she drove the car out of the small lane Dr. Churchouse appeared in what was presumably an official car from Harwell. They waved to him, he waved back.

Lilburne, somnolent already, half lying in the back seat with his arm resting on a pile of luggage, wondered if Dr. Churchouse, rid temporarily of outsiders and the English, would revert on entering the house to his native Germany.

Would he put on a velvet smoking-cap, play Beethoven on the

gramophone, and drink his tea out of a beer-mug with a lid on it? Had he got a long decorated pipe and a pair of leather shorts hidden away for such secret occasions?

The afternoon was hot and sticky. The hedges flew by, the scents of the countryside came in through the open windows and sunshine roof.

Lilburne realized that the peaceful music-loving image was wrong. Dr. Churchouse was a Prussian, not a Bavarian. Probably at this moment he was striding about in breeches and field boots, his monocle screwed in his eye, cutting at the furniture with a cavalry sabre.

That was rather how Lilburne had hoped he would be; he looked at the back of Mrs. Churchouse's genteel English head and saw the Churchouses' placid spaniel cowering before its master who, wearing a helmet taken from its hiding-place in the garden shed, once again shouted the harsh executive orders of the Uhlans of the Imperial Guard. The picture of the Kaiser and the Crown Prince taken from under the bed would stand by the gramophone which would bellow Wagner or, remembering the period, perhaps a Strauss waltz. Unter-Leutnant von Kirkhausen would click his booted heels.

Lilburne smiled to himself at his fancies. He closed his eyes. He couldn't tell how Mrs. Churchouse managed to stay awake and drive the car. Wagner or Strauss, he wasn't sure.

14

'A' COMPANY was no longer 'A' Company. Its members had become senior cadets. During their enforced weekend at Ypres before they started on the second stage of their training they realized the change in status and occupation.

As senior cadets they were divided into 'G' Squadron and 'E' Battery, according to whether they were destined for the Armoured Corps or the Artillery. Churchouse emerged as a senior under-officer, Arkwright, with two others, as a junior under-officer, with little strips of Austrian lace to be stitched to their battledress sleeves.

On the Saturday they all changed their barrack rooms. The R.A.C. cadets were issued with black berets and the R.A. cadets with blue ones. New white-celluloid circles were issued to be placed behind cap-badges. Any change of status in the Army must be signified by some tangible physical change, and just as at school it must be obvious that you have graduated to the Sixth Form, 'G' Squadron learned that it was no longer necessary to march in a body from lecture to lecture, a gentlemanly walk was permitted, and that if any cadet felt like it he might import a bicycle.

Many of the cadets, rather like schoolboys, looked back on their days as 'A' Company somewhat regretfully. They looked at one another, at the strange faces now among them, including three Jordanians, at their new headgear, at the unfamiliar lace knots on the sleeves of the under-officers, and thought of the basic O.C.T.U. as if it had been some rather pleasant prep school.

The military machine, however, grinds relentlessly on.

On Sunday evening a new C.S.M. appeared. Or, more properly, a squadron corporal-major in the Life Guards, called Greenaway. He appeared more mild than C.S.M. Dickens, but this again might have been the automatic deference shown to senior cadets.

Squadron Corporal-Major Greenaway produced a typewritten programme covering the next ten weeks on a day-to-day basis. The cadets gathered round the notice-board and flicked at its pages.

Two weeks were occupied by a thing called 'Trek', a fortnight's camp and training. For the rest, days and days seemed to be devoted to the study of tanks and armoured cars, their engines, their armament, and their wireless sets. Films, lectures, and demonstrations abounded. There were tests and examinations. Lilburne eyed a sheet and saw more clearly what he had thought he had seen, 'Ten-Mile Endurance Test'. He took no further interest in the programme.

Others found that there were still periods devoted to games and P.T., but the overall picture seemed obvious. The Army had tested these men's characters, endurance, courage, and initiative sufficiently in the six weeks' basic period. The object now was to give them the technical training for their trade.

Arkwright started to turn the pages back thoughtfully. 'Every day,' he said, 'sometimes twice a day, we have a thing called P.O.P. rehearsal. What's that?'

S.C.M. Greenaway, who still stood in the background, answered him. 'Passing-out parade rehearsal, of course. Under the R.S.M. every day until you're perfect.'

Apparently the post-graduate course was not to be entirely technical.

'G' Squadron continued throughout the enforced working weekend to prepare itself for the tasks to come. Or rather the authorities prepared 'G' Squadron.

Large ruled notebooks were issued. Scribbling pads with plastic covers, pamphlets on tank gunnery and tactics. Diagrams of tank engines, two sets of denim overalls, and pairs of goggles.

Soon the 'G' Squadron barrack room began to look like a rear area of a supply line for some great battle of the Second World War. The collection of all this military impedimenta had its effect on the cadets. They began to brace themselves, to think in warlike terms. At last they were to get to grips with the machinery of war. They saw themselves mastering the complicated arts of strategy and tactics, of familiarizing themselves with trajectories and muzzle velocities. Each one in his mind's eye saw himself, oil- and dust-stained, directing a troop of tanks through some complicated battle manœuvre.

'A' Company with its emphasis on boots and rifles and square-bashing was a thing of the past. They all felt they were now on the threshold of what they had chosen the Armoured Corps for.

The romance of the line of armoured vehicles lurching down a road, the small pennants on their wireless aerials fluttering in the breeze, the crackle of dramatic decisive orders coming over the wireless, the roar of the guns, the cracking of the co-ax machine guns. The speed of manœuvre, the excitement of the long march, the armoured thrust, the tanks bucketing over rough country. The dirty faces under their black berets transversed by the band of their headsets—confident of their knowledge of the powerful, death-dealing machines they controlled so expertly.

On Monday morning 'G' Squadron marched to the square and took up its new place on the right of the line. The rest of the Officer Cadet School stretched to its left. At the rear stood, gleaming and twinkling, a band.

R.S.M. Muxlow, sworded, and with his pace-stick under his arm, appeared. The drill adjutant walked his horse on to the square.

R.S.M. Muxlow addressed 'G' Squadron and 'E' Battery.

'You are now senior cadets,' he yelled, 'and that means something. From now until you pass out every morning, save for un-avoidable interruptions,' the R.S.M. grimaced at the thought, 'you will drill as you have never drilled before.'

'G' Squadron looked dumbly to its front. Its collective vision of the romance of armoured warfare faded.

'You may learn about tanks and guns,' screamed Muxlow, 'and mechanical contraptions of that sort. Works of the devil,' Muxlow waved his stick, 'but here you will learn to look like soldiers.

'Now,' said R.S.M. Muxlow—he braced himself. What followed was indescribable. The cadets of course had heard R.S.M. Muxlow's voice before, but now they heard it raised to sound over the noise of the band.

Under its direction the parade marched, counter-marched, advanced in review order, right formed and left formed, sloped, and presented and marched past until feet ached and sweat poured down faces.

Not only was the whole thing noisier on the basis of the competition between Muxlow and the band, but the intensity had increased. Sergeant-majors scurried about taking names left, right, and centre, under-officers bawled their orders as if to rupture their throats.

Even the drill adjutant, that lofty, distant being, perhaps infected by this, joined in. With drawn sword—so much for the pamphlets on technicalities—he rode with the parade, making his salute to an imaginary general on the saluting base. 'Look into the inspecting officer's eyes,' yelled R.S.M. Muxlow. Bishop Berkeley's theories on reality would have appealed to him.

The drill adjutant returned his sword to the carry, his horse edged to the left. Officer-Cadet Townshend, who hated horses, edged away. The drill adjutant pulled gently to his left.

'No, no,' yelled Muxlow, 'the dressing.' The band crashed into 'The Banner of St. George'.

'What is this punishment for?' asked the Jordanian cadet on Lilburne's right. Lilburne wisely kept his face to the front. The

Jordanian's name was written with some difficulty on to a millboard carried by S.C.M. Greenaway.

The heels hit the ground, the arms swung, the rifles jerked, backs straightened, and the sweat poured.

The parade halted with a resounding crash; the band thumped and was silent.

R.S.M. Muxlow closed in on 'G' Squadron. The intricacies of the Merlin engine or the range and trajectory of the 20-pounder might never have been.

'Gentlemen,' said Muxlow, 'you are typical of the decline of the British Army. Its deportment, its bearing, its pride, its drill are going down the drain.

'Only the other day I was standing in Upshott High Street when a funeral procession passed by. I saw two guardsmen and before my very eyes they saluted,' he paused, 'independently!

'Gentlemen,' his voice rose, 'if I'd been the bastard in the box I'd have raised the lid and shouted, "As you were."'

The last three words were shouted, the cadets smiled despite themselves. One unfortunate cadet in the rear rank sprang to attention. S.C.M. Greenaway wrote his name down on his millboard.

'That's the British Army today,' said Muxlow. 'A general decline. But you gentlemen will not—repeat not—be allowed to go down the drain. Eventually when you march up the steps I shall be proud of you.'

R.S.M. Muxlow looked at his watch with a quick drill movement. 'There will now be a break of five minutes. After that——' he stopped. 'Squadron Corporal-Major Greenaway, there's a cadet in the rear rank with an idle cap-badge. Officer-Cadet MacNeil it is. Get hold of him.'

Greenaway sprang to attention and looked at the rear rank with the eagerness of a pointer.

'Officer-Cadet MacNeil not on parade, sir. Reported sick this morning, sir.'

'Well, take the name of the cadet next to him.'

'Sir!'

R.S.M. Muxlow moved majestically to the other end of the parade. Lilburne looked at the Jordanian on his right. The dusky face gleamed with sweat. 'In Jordan this would not be allowed,' he said.

Lilburne felt savage, his battledress blouse chafed him under the armpits, his right hand bled from a mistimed slap to his rifle. He turned to Ransome on his left. 'You know, George, that girl Jo.'

'Yes.'

'What you told me about wearing black stockings—well, you were wrong. She doesn't.'

Ransome stared to his front, and muttered something unprintable out of the corner of his mouth.

'Parade,' yelled R.S.M. Muxlow. The future leaders of Britain's mechanized army straightened their backs, jerked their heels, and brought their right hands smartly down on their rifles.

As anyone who has read a general's memoirs will know, in every great military battle or exercise there is a plan, a grand design.

This of course is not always obvious to the participants, the individual soldiers taking part. Their view of the battle is of necessity fragmentary and episodic, sometimes merely chaotic.

This situation has sometimes given rise to complaints from the rank and file. Nevertheless it would seem to be of the nature of military exercises, for though apparently the commander, even in retrospect, always knew what he was doing and what was happening, others did not.

So it was with 'G' Squadron at Ypres O.C.S. The grand design was that they should be trained in the technique of armoured troop-leading. Their view of that training was however that despite constant activity only isolated unrelated incidents stood out in their minds.

The kaleidoscopic character of those weeks was perhaps not surprising, Lilburne reflected, when one realized that a great deal of the technical training was carried out literally in the dark.

The British Army has for a long time been sold on the idea of the instructional film. There are films which explain with the use of animated models how the breech of the 20-pounder gun works and how a tank engine works. There are films which show how to clear a minefield, or hide four tanks in a wood. Films explain how to advance, retreat, consolidate, and indeed every aspect of strategy and tactics save surrender.

The cadets in 'G' Squadron consequently found themselves plunged into a world of cinemas and darkened lecture-rooms. The whirr of projectors was constantly in their ears. In the breaks between films they were allowed out for five minutes to blink like pit ponies in the unaccustomed glare of the daylight. They smoked cigarettes and returned to darkness again.

Arkwright calculated that of the forty hours per week spent in training thirty were spent in darkness, the ten remaining hours being either P.T. or drill under the redoubtable R.S.M. Muxlow.

The ratio may well have been an exaggeration but the general impression was strong. Most cadets' mental vision was filled with the shapes from the rather erratic cartoons and the figures from the woodenly acted documentaries.

Although the film is part of modern life it is perhaps just that fact that limits its effectiveness as a means of imparting information. Modern youth, when it sees a film, expects to be entertained.

Lilburne found he was not; taken from a drill square after a punishing hour of physical effort, in the darkness of the lecture-room he would fall asleep. He would awake to see a cartoon of the breech-locking mechanism functioning smoothly. Through half-opened eyes he would see the extractors engage the shellcase, the breech would open smoothly again. Lilburne's eyes would close again.

It was during one of these cinema periods that the Cubes arrived.

A door was opened, a few whispered instructions, and three large white-uniformed figures moved into the front row.

Churchouse had one of these directly in front of him. He strained his eyes in the dark. A bull neck with a luxuriant growth of oily curly black hair surmounted shoulders thick with gold lace. Gold aiguilettes disappeared under a fleshy arm, a flash of a ring or two, and a gold-striped arm was stretched along the chair-backs. Churchouse smelt Chanel No. 5 and a powerful hairwash.

The film ended, the lights went on. Lilburne blinked and 'G' Squadron paraded outside under the gaze of three Central American generals. With them was an A.D.C. with a large camera. S.C.M. Greenaway appeared. 'G' Squadron marched to the square followed at a more leisurely pace by the Cubes—everybody assumed they were Cubans.

On the square stood R.S.M. Muxlow, slightly smaller than the senior Cuban general. The Commandant, the second in command, and a dismounted drill adjutant hovered in the background.

R.S.M. Muxlow began to scream, 'G' Squadron obediently performed military evolutions. The A.D.C. rushed about taking pictures with his camera. The Commandant joined the Cuban generals. They chatted, 'G' Squadron halted and fixed bayonets with a disciplined clatter.

The A.D.C. trotted to the middle of the square, went down on one knee, shifted the gold lace on his shoulders, and trained his camera on the saluting base. The Commandant nodded to the drill adjutant, the drill adjutant signalled to R.S.M. Muxlow with his riding-whip.

'G' Squadron began to march past in slow time. Churchouse gave the 'eyes right', the fattest Central American raised his hand to his gold-bedecked peaked cap. The A.D.C. took pictures furiously.

'G' Squadron marched off the square and returned to a film on tactics under nuclear attack. Most of the cadets were of the opinion that the senior Cube had been smoking a cigar when he took the salute.

A permanent regime of films tempered with drill could not of course continue. After three weeks the tempo changed. The films disappeared, to be replaced by demonstrations and exercises. The drill, of course, remained.

The cadets now found themselves standing round guns and engines while glib W.O. and N.C.O. instructors rapidly reeled off technicalities.

Ransome alone seemed happy, glorying in using expressions such as 'breech-mechanism actuating shaft' which he seemed to have learned by heart. Lilburne was particularly depressed by it all, especially as each instructor began his lecture by saying, 'Now you're all familiar with the working of this equipment from the films you've seen.'

It was after a session on the miniature range where cadets fired a .22 mounted to coincide with the controls in a tank turret at model tanks set out in a sandpit that Arkwright took Lilburne by the arm.

'Charles,' he said, 'are you going over to tea?'

'Yes, of course.'

'Do you mind if I have a word with you as we go over?'

Lilburne, surprised by this formality, looked hard at Arkwright. 'No, of course not, Peter. Anything wrong?'

'Well, yes, I got a telegram from home today. My brother, he was in the 60th and attached to the Gurkhas, has been killed in Malaya.'

'Oh dear, I am sorry.'

'Killed in an ambush, apparently.' Arkwright seemed to be intent on keeping his voice very matter-of-fact. 'Automatic fire, killed immediately. A letter from the colonel followed the telegram.'

'Have you had a word with the squadron-leader?'

'No, there's no point. I don't want leave or anything. They're burying John, they're burying him out there.'

'Oh, I see.'

'Trouble is, my mother has written saying I should resign here and ask for a home-posting on compassionate grounds, but I can't do that, can I?'

'Hardly, Peter. Anyway, what's the point? You may go abroad as an officer or you may stay at home. What does your father think?'

'My father died two years ago. You see, I am, as it were, the only one left.'

'Well, look, Peter. Get a week's leave and see your mother and explain that it doesn't make any difference whether you're commissioned or not.'

'She's worried that I might go to Malaya as well. She seems to think I've got a better chance of staying at home as an other rank.'

'Well, I should explain it to her.'

'All right, I'll do that, but you think I should stay here?'

Lilburne didn't really know why he was so sure. 'Oh, certainly,' he said.

'Good,' said Arkwright, 'I think you're right.'

Arkwright came back from his five days' leave at the end of the gunnery course just in time for a visit to Larkhill.

He nodded to Lilburne in the coach. 'All right,' he said. Lilburne smiled and nodded back.

He wondered why he had been so strong in his opinion. Probably Arkwright had made up his mind, anyway.

The trip to Larkhill was by way of a treat for senior cadets. A coach had been laid on instead of the usual army lorries, a packed lunch had been provided, and all cadets had been given permission to wear shoes rather than boots and gaiters. In unaccustomed luxury, 'G' Squadron felt it had been commissioned already.

At Larkhill they found themselves placed with groups of officers round a deep wide valley, in the bottom of which groups of tanks moved slowly. To 'G' Squadron's right a roped-off enclosure contained a score of red-tabbed senior officers. Just before the demonstration was to begin a company of Sandhurst cadets moved in on 'G' Squadron's left.

The two companies, one professional, the other merely temporary and amateur, looked at each other in curiosity and dislike. Lilburne looked at a programme he had been handed. It read:

Demonstration I Destruction of tanks by 25-pdr. field guns.
Demonstration II Destruction of tanks by anti-tank gun Mark VII.
Demonstration III Destruction of tanks by infantry armed with rifle and bayonet.
Demonstration IV Destruction of tanks by rocket-firing aircraft.

'G' Squadron, all destined to soldier in tanks or armoured cars, watched amazed and horrified while crewless tanks were moved into position and then bombarded by hideously accurate artillery fire. Then a small group of infantrymen, supporting a weapon that looked like a gaspipe with legs, crawled forward and calmly blew the tracks off the nearest tank.

Finally the aircraft. Everyone ducked instinctively as the rocket-carrying jets flew low into the valley. A swish, and the rockets detached themselves and swooped in groups of four at the tanks. A roar and a flash of sparks, and palls of black smoke hung over their turrets. Two of them began to burn furiously.

An officer appeared and spoke to Churchouse and the Sandhurst senior under-officer. 'Tea,' shouted Churchouse and pointed to a large tent at the end of the valley. Both companies moved towards it on parallel courses.

Arkwright looked towards the V.I.P. enclosure and caught the eye of a brigadier looking benevolently down on these young lads going off to their tea.

Each company quickened their pace as if engaged in a race. Lilburne on the fringe met an 11th Hussar major in his gorgeous cherry-coloured trousers, picking his way carefully through the mud as he came up from the valley.

He acknowledged Lilburne's salute and looked at his cap-badge. 'In the wrong business, I'm afraid,' he said.

'G' Squadron and the Sandhurst company met at the door of the tea tent and poured in in a double stream. Inside, a trestle table with urns and cups and plates of sandwiches and cakes stretched the length of the tent. Two white-coated N.A.A.F.I. girls presided. Both companies, trained to attack, marched forward. MacNeil found himself being jostled by a tiny Sandhurst cadet. He looked at him. 'Hello, Scott,' he said, 'haven't seen you since school.'

'No,' said Scott, shoving more violently, 'how are you?' A bun whistled over their heads. MacNeil pushed Scott hard in the chest and he fell backwards into the crowd.

Someone hit Lilburne in the back. His tea slopped over his battledress. He threw the cup and saucer at his attacker. 'Come on, "G" Squadron,' shouted Churchouse, throwing cakes from a plate. Three Sandhurst cadets pushed Cresswell under a table and forced sandwiches down his neck.

Someone knocked over a tea-urn. The two N.A.A.F.I. girls crawled out under the bottom of the tent.

It ended as soon as it began. A trestle table creaked and broke under a crush of bodies. Ransome on the ground began to pull up the pegs holding the guy-ropes. The tent lurched alarmingly and a part of the roof fell in.

The fighting inside became quieter. Cadets streamed out of the entrance. They collected in two groups and scowled at one another. They started to straighten their uniforms and adjust their berets. Churchouse looked at his watch. They began to move off to their respective coaches.

What neither side could understand was why no one had

interfered. Presumably the officers were fully occupied in entertaining the V.I.P.s in the mess.

Returned to Ypres, 'G' Squadron concentrated for two weeks on 'D and M', Driving and Maintenance. Clad in overalls the cadets clustered round engines and endeavoured to get as much oil and grease on their hands as possible.

Many thought about the fight in the tea tent, but nothing happened. Presumably higher authority had decided to treat it all as a commendable display of high spirits.

Arkwright remembered the brigadier he had noticed in the V.I.P. enclosure and saw him saying to his colleagues: 'Young fellahs, you know. No harm in a bit of horseplay, dammit. When I was at Sandhurst we burnt down the stables. . . .'

Doubtless Arkwright's character-reading was accurate, for no complaint was ever heard.

15

LILBURNE woke with the same feeling of foreboding that he had tried to dispel on going to bed. For weeks now as he carried out his daily, fairly happy, tasks as a senior cadet he had put it firmly at the back of his mind. Slowly, however, the concertina-like effect of the training programme had brought the day nearer. Now it had arrived, today was the day of the Endurance Test—more popularly the 'ten-mile bash'. He knew he could not run ten miles to save his life.

Up till now Ypres had been fairly tolerable; a lot of square-bashing, a lot of fairly straightforward P.T., and more interviews than seemed really necessary. Indeed, looking back, interviews of one sort or another seemed to predominate, and their terrors disappeared after the first one or two. Now one was required actually to do something. A pleasant manner and a show of assumed keenness was not enough.

He couldn't really see why it was so vital for someone who was for the rest of his army life to travel about in a tank or an armoured car to be able to run ten miles in full infantryman's kit. He thought wryly of the Cockney recruit to the Navy who when asked if he could swim said, 'Why, ain't you got no boats?'

If it was courage that was being tested why not try something within everyone's physical capabilities?

He looked round the barrack-room. Churchouse was his usual impassive self. Arkwright looked cheerful as he collected his razor,

soap, and towel, even Ransome still lying in bed seemed unconcerned by his impending fate. Perhaps they could all run like deer.
Lilburne wondered what would happen if he feigned sickness or
better still asked to see the Commandant and put it to him man to
man, 'I could never run at school, I cannot now, are you going to
throw me out because of this alone?' Could the Commandant, all
silk handkerchiefs and elegant tailoring, run ten miles? Anyhow,
why only officers? In the ranks he had never been asked to run ten
miles.

Ransome looked across at him. 'Bloody awful day, Charles, ten-
mile bash this afternoon.'

Lilburne began to get out of bed. 'I know I can't do it so it doesn't
matter, quite hopeless.'

Ransome looked at him more closely. 'It's all a matter of getting
your second wind, you know, after that it's all right.'

'Look, George, everyone has been telling me that since I was
about fourteen. We used to run at school, the whole school, once a
week. It never happened to me, I was always last. I only got
out of it when I became head of my house and invented other
duties.'

He looked at Ransome's helpful face. 'There's nothing I can do,
so let's forget about it, shall we?' Within the military framework
there was a limit to how far one could go in the confession of
failure, even to Ransome.

He dressed in shirt and trousers and went off to shave. As he
shaved he tried deep-breathing exercises. He got lather up his nose
and cut his chin and his feeling of hopelessness increased.

The morning passed automatically: the usual drill parade, a
film, a lecture, these all seemed unreal. Only during P.T. did his
mind come to life. What if he fell from the wall-bars or deliberately
vaulted badly over the horse? Would he be excused if he injured
himself sufficiently? Would they just let him recover and then let
him do the run on his own? In the queue waiting to vault over the
horse Lilburne decided that all he would succeed in doing was to

give himself a few painful bruises and thus make his showing in the afternoon even worse than it would be normally.

At lunch he ate sparingly, eating with a group of cadets he normally hardly spoke to—he felt he couldn't stand the company of his ordinary companions. Their conversation and cheerfulness would be unbearable; worse still, if he revealed his fears, to have to listen to their expressions of sympathy or offers of advice.

Accidentally, though, he fell in with Churchouse as they walked back to the barrack-room to put on full kit and collect their rifles. Lilburne lit a cigarette.

'Shouldn't do that, Charles,' said Churchouse. 'Spoil your wind.'

Lilburne drew heavily on it. 'Won't make the slightest difference, I'll never finish the course.'

Churchouse smiled. Lilburne could have kicked him; would no one realize that the one thing he could not do was run ten miles?

In the barrack-room, as everyone changed seemingly gaily into shirtsleeve order and then started to strap on pack and cartridge-pouches, Lilburne stood apart, his stomach becoming cold and constricted. He changed quickly and had another cigarette. Could he assume some crippling illness or even a stomach complaint at this late stage? He certainly felt ill. As if mesmerized he joined the others in their walk to the marshalling point.

Two P.T. sergeants bundled them into a truck and they were driven out of the camp area to one of those typical, sandy, gorse-covered stretches that abound by the roadside near Upshott. Lilburne stepped gingerly out of the truck as if it were a tumbril, the cadets gathered round a white flag on a post. Beside it stood Major Stainton, the new squadron-leader, aloof and disdainful, leaning on a wooden trestle table which supported a millboard, a few pencils, and a blue-and-white Penguin classic. Major Stainton waved a languid hand. 'C'on, Sarn't-Major,' he said.

A gruff-voiced P.T. sergeant-major took over. As he talked he bounced, flexing his leg muscles and lowering his head, as if about to charge the assembled cadets. 'The course is all laid out with white flags like these.' He pointed so that all could digest and assimilate the nature, size, and texture of this particular white flag. 'Some country, some road, nice easy run in a circle ending up here.' He pointed precisely at a piece of Hampshire earth at his feet. 'Then from here we go on to the range and you fire your ten rounds.' He paused. 'That's not my job, of course.' He smiled so as to dissociate himself from such ignoble arts.

His bouncing became more pronounced. 'My two sergeants,' he indicated them, 'will accompany you round.' The two sergeants bounced slightly to show their willingness. 'And one final word, gentlemen, there are no short cuts that are worth while.

'Right, gentlemen.' He inhaled and exhaled to demonstrate his pectoral muscles. 'Line up in two ranks across the road and we start precisely at 1400.' Lilburne shuffled into the second line, hoisted his rifle on its sling across his back, and tried vainly to look eager. Out of the corner of his eye he saw that Major Stainton had already seated himself behind the table and opened his book.

'Go,' yelled the sergeant-major.

The crowd pushed and shoved and broke into an uneasy trot. Lilburne sucked in his stomach muscles and, with an exaggerated assumption of the easy loping stride of the trained athlete, found himself among the first half-dozen for about three hundred yards. His tightly clenched mouth then came open of its own accord, his boots began to hurt him, and he fell ignominiously to the rear. He braced himself into a little more effort as the two sergeants idled beside him and then passed him. Ahead a snake of khaki figures turned off the road at a white flag and began to stretch along a rough track across a low hill.

Lilburne pulled at the sling of his rifle, trying to prevent the trigger-guard and magazine from digging into his back with every stride he took; he found himself running lop-sided and left the sling alone and continued to receive metallic jolts to the spinal column. He half walked, half ran off the road on to the track which was baked hard by the sun. His mouth was now permanently open, his breath was coming in great gasps, and he had an uneasy feeling that his leg-bones were projecting through his heels. He knew that if he stopped now he would not be able to run again; he wiped the sweat out of his eyes and toiled up the hill, his boots clumsily kicking up spurts of dust.

At the top he saw the other cadets dimly in the distance, more strung out now but still moving steadily; another white flag indicated the way across country towards some farm buildings. The track had petered out now and he found himself following a line of gorse bushes and stumbling over small hillocks and mounds.

How far had he run now; two miles, three? His foot hit another hummock and he came to a halt. It was no good; he stopped and wiped his brow with his handkerchief. He found himself wondering if Major Stainton could run ten miles, or even one. Could it be possible that any of their impossibly indolent instructors had been forced to do this? He walked on breathing gratefully and a little more gently, his feet ached and he felt he was going to be sick. He began to doubt if he could walk the distance.

It all seemed so grossly unfair. He thought he was an average soldier, reasonably competent now and reasonably fit, certainly as strong as some of the weedier members of the squadron who were now running miles ahead of him. Could they actually send him back to his unit as a failure just for not being able to run?

Perhaps he should have prepared himself by taking practice runs each evening—he dismissed the idea as ridiculous. Perhaps he just wasn't good enough. In a war, in actual fighting, if people were shooting at him, would he be able to run ten miles? What about all those boring Buchan heroes of his boyhood who were doing this sort of thing daily? He straightened his back, closed his mouth, and trying to breathe steadily through his nose, forced himself to stagger towards a farmyard.

A white flag fluttered on a post stuck into a crevice in a wall, a farmer in Wellingtons stood by a door and watched his approach incuriously. Lilburne eyed a black-and-white collie of unpleasant appearance and ran on, a dozen or so hens darted about in his path and scattered as he came nearer.

One hen scuttled by his feet and nearly tripped him up. A sudden vigorous thump to his right calf. He stopped and turned to find himself confronted by an enormous Rhode Island Red cockerel, its plumage fluffed out and its wings raised. It half jumped forwards; Lilburne looked at it warily; surely one couldn't run away from a bird? He gave a rather ineffectual 'shoo' and waved his hand at it. Immediately one of his fingers was seized, and with a flap of its wings the bird was digging its feet into the skin above his knees. Lilburne tried to grab one of the flapping wings and missed but somehow threw the agitated bundle of spiky feathers, beak, and claws away from him. He sucked at his finger, which was bruised and bleeding. The bird, its eyes gleaming and beak agape, took up its former stance, head thrust out, wings upraised, and feet splayed. Lilburne had never seen such a large cockerel before; he thought about kicking it and wondered if it might jump up and peck at one's eyes. He unslung his rifle, and holding it like a cricket bat advanced.

'Oy!' A shout from the farmer. Lilburne, keeping one eye on the bird, swivelled slightly. 'You don't have to kill him, you know.' The farmer came towards them slowly. Lilburne with a dirty look at the cockerel backed to join him.

'Bloody bird bit me,' he said.

'Oh, he will, he will, bags of spirit, it's the game in them, you know.' The farmer seemed proud of the fact, he smiled indulgently at the cockerel which had begun to strut about in a circle.

'Hurts like hell.' Lilburne felt that his alliterative remarks were receiving little sympathy. He bound his handkerchief round his finger; could you get poisoned by such wounds? he wondered.

'What are all you blokes doing today?' asked the farmer. Clearly the subject of the cockerel was closed. Lilburne came back to earth.

'Running ten miles,' he said, 'and don't ask me why because I don't know.'

The farmer seemed to be about forty, with a pleasant face. Lilburne thought he would probably have been in the war.

'You're last, I suppose?'

Lilburne was about to say that his brush with the cockerel hadn't improved his chances of winning, but thought better of it.

'Never could run this far,' he said. 'I never get my second wind. Whole family just the same, must be hereditary; my brother had just the same trouble when he was in the Army.'

Why he had invented a brother he couldn't tell, somehow it made the whole thing more convincing. The farmer continued to gaze at him.

'Where do you go from here?'

'Round the hill,' Lilburne gestured as he started to re-sling his rifle, 'and then back, about five miles.'

'Would a lift across country on my tipper help?'

Lilburne hesitated. 'They check us, I think,' he said. What had he got to lose, anyway, he would never finish the course normally. Could he magnify the cockerel incident?

The farmer must have been a mind-reader. 'Old Rufus must have delayed you a bit, I'll get the tipper out and drive you across, then you'll meet up with your chums on the road.'

Lilburne stood still and tried to think. He would never get round, he knew, and perhaps they weren't watching the check-points, anyway. He nodded his head mutely. In a matter of moments he was half sitting, half lying in the body of the little vehicle and the farmer was driving it across country at a bone-shuddering speed.

The farmer drove vigorously, grinning at Lilburne in an impersonal sort of way as if he were regarding one of his own bullocks. Lilburne bounced about on the tipper and when he could grinned back. When they had gone a mile or so Lilburne began to shout what he would rather have whispered. That he would like to be

dropped a little short of the road. The farmer nodded compre-
hendingly, grinned, and said nothing. Over the scarcely discernible
track they bounded, until the telegraph poles were only a few
hundred yards off. The tipper stopped with a lurch, Lilburne
jumped off.

He began his thanks. 'My brother, in the Welsh Guards, eventually killed, poor chap, at Cassino,' he said on the spur of the
moment. The tipper was turning, why had he said that—to gain
sympathy or to excuse himself? The farmer waved a hand and was
off. Had the Welsh Guards been at Cassino? It sounded probable.

Lilburne approached the road circumspectly, luckily for he was
just in time to lie flat in some bushes as a straggling group of cadets
trotted wearily past. No sergeants. Lilburne was up and on to the
road and panting in the rear. The last man was Ransome, Lilburne
caught up with him. They panted along together.

'How much farther?' gasped Lilburne; he was beginning to
wonder if he could manage even now.

' 'Bout a mile,' said Ransome. 'What happened to you? Thought
you'd passed out like Meynell. Stitch?'

'Stitch,' said Lilburne, he was slowing down again.

A white flag and some khaki figures. They passed a civilian
youth and his girl as if they weren't members of the same species
and ran the last hundred yards in some sort of style.

Major Stainton ticked off their names on his millboard. 'You
two appear to be last,' he said. His eyes were straying back to his
book.

'What about Meynell?' said the sergeant-major. Lilburne stayed
silent.

Ransome, who looked as if he was going to be sick at any
moment, gulped, 'He fainted, I think, the two P.T.I.s are looking
after him.'

'Send a truck, Sarn't-Major,' said Major Stainton from his book.

A corporal went running off to an attendant truck. The driver
put down the *Mirror* and started the engine.

A thin intense sergeant, dressed properly in clean battledress, appeared, saluted Major Stainton's bent head, and shouted, 'To the range double,' and himself ran off in that direction. The cadets stumbled behind him.

'Trail arms,' yelled the sergeant. The cadets tore at their rifle-slings in the effort of trying to negotiate them over their packs. Ransome stopped and started to vomit.

Lilburne fell gratefully but painfully into a sandbagged firing position. Clips of ammunition were handed out. On the shouted order Lilburne began to cram the rounds down against the magazine spring.

A pair of boots appeared by his shoulders. 'What's the handkerchief for?' asked the sergeant.

Lilburne looked at the bloodstained and dirty bandage he had made. 'I was bitten by . . .' he began. He tore it off and continued to press down the rounds.

'Fire in your own time,' said the voice above him.

Lilburne's eyes focussed vaguely on a black-and-white target and he pulled the trigger. He fired five rounds in rapid succession carelessly, not minding as he bruised his shoulder with the recoil.

'You're not trying, Cadet,' said the sergeant. 'Terrible shooting. What would you do in a real battle?'

'Use the bayonet,' muttered Lilburne into a sandbag, pulling the trigger and working the bolt happily.

16

THE weeks wore on, and as the course came nearer its end it seemed to accelerate. Soon there would only be a week before the fortnight's trek and then a week before they passed out.

The incidents became telescoped. Junior cadets began to look younger. Townshend was relegated to another squad and began the course all over again. Lloyd broke his arm on the assault course. The squadron-leader interviewed Lilburne and seriously advised him to go to bed earlier and get more sleep during the night. Cresswell was refused leave to go to Ascot.

Churchouse borrowed a horse and, for a bet, rode it through a barrack-room. An enterprising firm in Upshott let out wireless sets on hire to various groups of cadets. Insurance men arrived and talked to cadets about the dangers of leaving their kit uninsured when commissioned. Fires and floods apparently abounded and fifty per cent of every regiment's officers were thieves or pickpockets.

Tailors began to arrive from London to measure cadets for uniforms, and in their wake regimental colonels or their representatives to assess cadets' suitability for the regiments which wore the uniforms. Churchouse and Cresswell alone travelled to London to be interviewed by the commanding officer of the Household Cavalry.

Life became more leisurely. Cadets, in twos and threes, anxious to break with the traditional cinema and meal in Aldershot, began to take trips to the theatre in London. In a rather Edwardian manner whatever theatre they visited they saw a 'show'.

Ransome began to consider the dwindling balance in his post office savings book. Lilburne, suffering from the after-effects of the ten-mile bash, gave up smoking for at least three days.

A cricket match was arranged; Parker, to everyone's surprise, turned out to be a skilled fast bowler. Major Stainton appeared on the ground in immaculate flannels and boating jacket and an M.C.C. tie and dark glasses, and read a novel throughout. A few days later many cadets were wearing dark glasses.

Although work might seem to be easier, and more and more groups of cadets, attired in felt hats, hacking jackets, and cavalry twill trousers were able to leave barracks early and return late, one trial still remained, its ardour unabated—the daily session on the drill square. One might be a senior cadet, almost certain to be commissioned in about three weeks' time, but one was still required to sweat and stamp at the behest of R.S.M. Muxlow. It was just before they departed to Castlemartin for their fortnight's final exercise that 'G' Squadron experienced what was later called 'Muxlow's mad morning'.

Some said that Muxlow himself had been publicly rebuked by the drill adjutant on some previous parade, some that he had been insulted by having to drill the camp permanent staff of clerks and cooks before breakfast.

Whatever the reason—other theories ranged from liver to matrimonial difficulties—R.S.M. Muxlow was obviously not in a good temper. The whole morning from nine to twelve was devoted to drill, perhaps as a send-off to the senior cadets lest they become unsoldierly lost in the Welsh countryside.

The cause was conjectural, the purpose doubtful, but the effect was obvious. 'G' Squadron suffered.

There were warnings, slight rumblings of thunder before the storm broke.

'This morning, gentlemen,' R.S.M. Muxlow had said, 'we shall excel ourselves; we shall drill with the band and to the beat of the drum.' His voice rose with pure pleasure as he described how the second or executive part of the order would not be given but would be supplied by a tap on a kettledrum.

A demonstration was given. R.S.M. Muxlow yelled 'Slope' and instead of following that with 'arms' there was a sharp bang from an attendant drummer.

Next, Muxlow proudly produced a metronome handed to him by one of the company sergeant-majors. He placed it before 'G' Squadron, gave it a smart flick, and set it in motion. It ticked loudly, regularly, and rhythmically.

'G' Squadron looked at it, fascinated.

'Can any cadet tell me,' shouted Muxlow, 'what this is?'

Parker stood to attention in the front rank. 'Sir,' he said, 'it's a metronome.'

'Nonsense,' yelled Muxlow, 'it's an instrument for measuring the pace of marching.'

He marched off to take up his position in the centre of the parade.

Perhaps even at this late hour all might have been well had it not been for the bandmaster.

R.S.M. Muxlow had only just begun to explain how the drummer and the metronome would conjoin to assist in the production of a higher standard of foot and arms drill when the band suddenly burst into 'My Boy Willie'.

Muxlow paused open-mouthed, his face turned plum colour. He made an effort. His voice soared over the noise made by thirty musicians. 'Mr. Denny,' he screamed, 'stop, stop, qui-et!'

'My Boy Willie' petered out in squawks and toots.

Mr. Denny, the bandmaster, a tiny spectacled full lieutenant, his baton delicately held between thumb and forefinger, blinked at R.S.M. Muxlow.

'So sorry,' he said. 'I didn't hear you, Mr. Muxlow.'

A leaf fell from a tree by the side of the square quite audibly. In the far distance a train hooted.

R.S.M. Muxlow stood still. The parade inhaled and exhaled. The metronome still ticked. The earth swung slantingly on its axis.

The next noise to come from R.S.M. Muxlow was a thing of beauty. It soared and broke like a hunting horn on a frosty winter morning. The cadets knew they were privileged to be hearing the music of the spheres. 'Parade . . .' sang R.S.M. Muxlow. The drummer knew instinctively that it was not for him to complete this order. His sticks remained poised in mid air. 'Shun!' yelled R.S.M. Muxlow. The siren song could not be resisted. Each foot crashed to the ground, precisely, beautifully, and simultaneously.

The parade continued. Lt. Bandmaster Denny turned towards the band. His face implored them not to play a wrong note.

The next victim was one C.S.M. Woodfall, a newly joined drill instructor. An hour had passed. The day was warm. 'G' Squadron, as the passing-out troop, had done twice as much drill as anyone else. They were flagging as they passed Woodfall.

'More swank!' he yelled. 'More swank, you're marching like a lot of bloody ruptured ducks.'

'Company Sergeant-Major Woodfall,' yelled Muxlow in his most terrible voice, 'come here.

'Halt the parade,' shouted Muxlow. 'Turn the cadets about.'

This done, in what he fondly imagined was a whisper, over-heard by the cadets with their backs to him some yards off, R.S.M. Muxlow spoke to the unfortunate Woodfall.

'For your information,' he said, 'officer-cadets will not be sworn at and will not—repeat not—be referred to as ruptured ducks, you horrible, bloody little man.' His voice rose to Caruso strength again. 'Get off my parade at the double.' The cadets were turned about in time to see a sergeant-major doubling away into the distance.

In the next hour the parade drilled and the metronome

measured inadequacies. 'G' Squadron slow-marched off the parade and returned perhaps some twenty times. The band accompanied them each time with 'Auld Lang Syne'.

The casualties were large. Two sergeants, three under-officers, and twenty-seven cadets were all doubled off the square towards the guardroom.

The band played a slow waltz for an inspection. Muxlow moved grandly along the rigid ranks scrutinizing the bearing of each cadet, a word here and a tap of the pace-stick there.

He adjusted Meynell's hand as it gripped his rifle. 'You're not awake, Cadet,' he growled. Meynell endeavoured to tighten muscles already tautened. Muxlow moved off. Suddenly he rounded on Meynell, pointing at him with his pace-stick.

'What tune's the band playing?' he shouted.

' "My Boy Willie", sir,' said Meynell brightly.

The twenty-eighth cadet was doubled off the parade.

At ten minutes to twelve the parade rested for five minutes before marching off. The band was silent. Muxlow moved to the left of the line and rested his hands on his pace-stick.

'Thank Christ!' Ransome heard S.C.M. Greenaway mutter.

'Squadron Corporal-Major Greenaway.' The roar of a wounded elephant.

'Sir!'

'There's a cadet in your squadron wearing brown gloves—brown gloves.'

'Sir!' Greenaway looked in desperation along the ranks.

Muxlow, perhaps fifty yards away, directed him.

'Not there. In the front rank. Are you blind? Brown gloves, I can see him.'

'Sir!' howled Greenaway piteously as he ran along the front rank.

'You've just passed him, get hold of him.' The wounded elephant was about to charge.

'Squadron Corporal-Major, you're idle.' The words were

spaced menacingly. 'The cadet second on your right, now. You must see him.' Exasperation sent the voice up an octave.

'Sir!'

One of the Jordanian cadets, grinning broadly, marched smartly one pace forward.

Lt. Bandmaster Denny raised his baton. The band broke into the march 'Imperial Echoes'.

There was no rebuke from R.S.M. Muxlow as the parade began to march off.

The train journey from Upshott to Castlemartin via London is a long one. To while away the time one can eat, smoke, sleep, or read a novel if one has been long-sighted enough to bring one. Arkwright, Churchouse, Lilburne, Ransome, and Cresswell and one middle-aged lady had done all these things. Lilburne, who had sat opposite her, had been forced to talk to the middle-aged lady about her dog. Now and then with an amused audience of four he had been obliged to talk to her about the Army, its hardships, and its rigours.

Outside, evening was approaching. Wales looked old-fashioned and peaceful. The train itself seemed to have become quieter. It moved slowly and almost circumspectly through the descending twilight.

It stopped gently at a small station. Ransome saw a board with an unpronounceable collection of consonants. The middle-aged lady gathered her bags around her. 'Well, I hope you enjoy your—er—camp,' she said to the carriage at large. She leant towards Lilburne. 'Tell me one thing, those bits of braid.' She pointed to the under-officers' knots on the sleeves of Churchouse and Arkwright. 'I know you are all cadets, but what do those mean?'

Ransome smiled. This had happened before in the Upshott train. Then Lilburne had said they were in a penal battalion. Ransome knew what was coming.

'Those cadets are in the band,' said Lilburne

'Thank you, ah yes, you will forgive my curiosity.' She smiled at Churchouse and Arkwright, who scowled at her.

'I hope that will help,' she said quickly, placing a pound note on Cresswell's knee and darting out of the carriage. Cresswell half rose as the train puffed and shook itself into motion.

'What the hell is that for?' he said.

'Is it for all of us?' asked Ransome.

'No, only for Cresswell,' said Lilburne.

'How the hell do you know?'

'Well,' said Lilburne, 'I told her at lunch-time that Alec was illegitimate and brought up in an orphanage and we all gave him five bob a week to help him pay for his uniform when he was commissioned.'

'False pretences,' said Arkwright, but Cresswell was already trying to throw Lilburne's beret out of the window.

At Castlemartin camp there are perfectly good, brick-built barracks but 'G' Squadron, perhaps to simulate active service, was to live in tents.

Beside their tent lines stood the tents of a unit of the Territorial Army, a rather fashionable Yeomanry regiment.

The air was peaceful, almost sleepy. In the distance could be sensed the sea. All round stretched the misty Pembrokeshire countryside, quiet and isolated.

A dozen speckled, immature gulls sat around on the tent-poles. Rabbits scampered a few yards off, now and then sitting up to look incuriously at the tents.

A cavalry sergeant-major from the permanent staff approached Churchouse.

'Get your chaps settled down,' he said. 'First parade 0800 when your officers will give you the form here.' He looked towards the Yeomanry. 'Don't bother about the T.A.,' he said. 'Tonight's their last night. They're off in the morning.'

'G' Squadron began to put their kit and their blankets into their tents. As they did so one or two Yeomanry officers in blues, chain-mail on their shoulders, yellow-striped tight overalls, spurs, and cross-belts appeared and watched them.

A young lieutenant stepped with some difficulty over the guy-ropes and across the grass to Ransome. 'You from Ypres?' he said.

Ransome stood to attention. 'Yes, sir.'

'Ghastly place. So's this, in those bloody tents. All one's kit gets rusty. Spurs, chain-mail, the lot.'

Ransome itched to say, 'Why wear them?'

'We'll be off in the morning. Dinner-night tonight, dining out the Colonel.'

Ransome endeavoured to look wise.

'What regiment are you going to?'

'I don't know yet, sir.'

'Ah,' said the lieutenant; he walked back to his companions, who were opening a gin-bottle.

Ransome, now properly trained, saluted his back.

Dining out the Colonel in the Yeomanry regiment was apparently a lengthy and rather curious business. For some hours the quiet Pembrokeshire night was rent with laughter, shouts, and singing. Thunderflashes and what sounded like a revolver were fired. A hunting horn wailed.

A midnight the cadets heard the field for a steeplechase being assembled. They looked out a few minutes later and saw a score of shadowy blue-clad figures heaving themselves confusedly over the Yeomanry tents.

Half an hour later four cadets sharing a tent were rudely awakened by a scarlet-faced major who burst in upon them. His chain-mail gleamed, his medals shone, his cross-belt glittered, but below his tunic he wore nothing save his socks.

'Got to hide,' he said. He waved a champagne-bottle vaguely. 'The sods.' Four subalterns entered, seized him, and carried him off, struggling and swearing.

A cheer went up from outside, one of the subalterns returned and grabbed the champagne-bottle.

Meynell was privileged a few minutes later to overhear a short conversation through his tent wall.

'My name is Major Stainton,' said a familiar dry voice. 'I order you to go to bed.'

'Have a drink,' shouted a voice.

'Though at present through no fault of my own I have no uniform to prove it, I am also a major,' went on another heavier voice, which slurred its sibilants, 'and I can tell you this. Unless you go to bed you too will be stripped naked and probably painted.'

A roar of approval greeted this last remark.

'Good night,' said Major Stainton.

Next morning the cadets of 'G' Squadron stood in front of the now deserted Yeomanry tents, while an even more laconic and intense Major Stainton explained the plan for the fortnight's training.

Again as in their basic training each cadet would have a period of command, but the exercises this time would be with armoured cars and there would be a final period of firing on the ranges.

This short announcement heralded a period of intense activity.

For ten days armoured cars rolled along the roads and lanes of Pembrokeshire. Maps were studied closely and the air was filled with wireless messages.

In the evening if there were no night exercises the cadets, too weary to visit cinema or pub, fell gratefully on to their beds.

At the end of the ten days 'G' Squadron moved to the ranges and their world became bounded by the sharp crack of two-pounders and the smell of oil and cordite. As if their lives depended on it cadets stood up in turrets and peered through binoculars and yelled range corrections at their fellows crouched in the gunner's seat and slammed shells into ever-open breeches.

Just before the weekend the Commandant arrived, and stood,

elegant and aloof, watching their efforts. The cadets, spurred on by his presence, redoubled their efforts, shouting louder and squinting more intently through their gun periscopes.

That evening the cadets were taken out to a nearby mess by the Commandant. He bought them beer and, while chatting amicably to groups in turn, congratulated them on their performance. Major Stainton told them how a friend of his had fashioned a regimental badge out of scraps of wire and cloth while in a Japanese prisoner-of-war camp. The cadets tried to look as if they had never heard of him before.

So far everyone had enjoyed themselves; dealing with armoured cars on a practical basis was so much easier than the theory at Ypres. In a fortnight even the slowest cadet had gained a wealth of knowledge. They all felt confident and experienced.

On the last Saturday, however, Major Stainton announced a treat he had organized as a relaxation from their labours. In a party they were to climb a local mountain. Ransome almost volunteered to clean the guns instead.

In the afternoon a truck took them to the foot of the mountain. Major Stainton was there already in shorts and heavy boots, flexing his leg muscles.

The party set out at a brisk walk over the gentle lower slopes. Soon they began to ascend more steeply. Churchouse was at their head. At the back were Ransome and Lilburne, who stumbled along muttering to each other.

'Thank God we can get a drink at the pub on the other side, Charles.'

'What gives you the idea we shall ever get there?'

They staggered on, getting farther and farther behind the main party.

Down a narrow track strode a tall rubicund bald man in his fifties. He wore shorts and an open-necked shirt.

'Good afternoon,' he said. He stood back for the two cadets.

'Splendid plan,' he said cheerfully as they passed him, 'giving lads like you a love of the mountains while you're training. You'll be back when you've left the Army.'

Lilburne gave him a sickly smile. 'I'm training to be a soldier, not a bloody goat,' said Ransome loudly.

Sticky and footsore, Lilburne and Ransome reached a ledge some hundreds of feet short of the summit. The mist swirled above their heads. The rest of 'G' Squadron were nowhere to be seen.

They looked at each other and began to descend the other side.

They stopped frequently to rest their legs and smoke cigarettes, so that dusk was approaching when they saw a white road running some hundred yards below them.

A solitary ancient motor-cycle combination appeared, chugging slowly round the bend. Lilburne and Ransome began to run, shouting and leaping over the uneven ground. The combination stopped. A face like a nut peered at them from under an ancient flying helmet.

'Could you give us a lift to the village?' panted Lilburne.

'Are you going to the village?' asked Ransome. Neither dared to attempt to pronounce the name.

'Yes,' said the motor-cyclist, 'do you want a lift?'

Both nodded dumbly. Ransome heaved himself clumsily into the sidecar. Lilburne sat behind the driver.

The combination chugged slowly along the lonely road. All around the silence stretched up to the mist-covered mountains.

'What are you doing here?' said the cyclist.

'Training,' said Lilburne.

'Proper 'orrid life, the Army, isn't it?'

'Yes.'

They covered a mile in silence.

'Tell me,' said the motor-cyclist, 'what are those white things on your lapels for?'

'It means we are cadets.'

'What's that?'

Lilburne raised his voice. 'We are cadets.'

'I heard you the first time—what are cadets?' said the cyclist. The lilt in his voice seemed to keep time with the engine.

'We're training to be officers.'

'Officers, is it?' the engine coughed as the man raised his voice, 'and here I am giving you a lift.

'I'll tell you this,' he half turned his head and the cycle veered to the right, 'all our officers in the Royal Welch Fusiliers were proper bastards.'

'We're going into the cavalry,' said Lilburne tactfully, looking anxiously at the handlebars.

'Ooh,' said the motor-cyclist, 'cavalry is it? Nasty stuck-up lot. Worse, much worse.'

He braked, and the combination stopped in the middle of the road. 'You two can bloody well walk the rest.'

Ransome and Lilburne, speechless, dismounted reluctantly.

'Cavalry officers, indeed.' The flying helmet shook in indignation. The combination moved off down the road.

'Hope he has a burst tyre,' said Lilburne.

Ransome shook his fist at the now accelerating motor-cycle. 'Wish I could swear in Welsh,' he muttered.

When they reached the village and the pub 'G' Squadron had finished its last round of drinks. Lilburne and Ransome joined them as they climbed up into the lorry.

'Missed your drink,' said Major Stainton.

'I see what that chap on the motor-bike meant,' said Ransome.

17

BACK in Upshott 'G' Squadron relaxed. A half-day written examination and their labours were over. A short revision course on the drill square and they began to hand in their kit. S.C.M. Greenaway fussed about, inspecting their uniforms for the passing-out parade. Inches of polish were reapplied to boots and the creases and stains of a fortnight under canvas were removed.

Officers' uniforms began to arrive from tailors, and Ransome had a brief moment of glory when the examination results were announced. He stood top of the list with the magnificent total of two hundred and ninety-eight out of a possible three hundred.

The evening before the passing-out parade Lilburne and Arkwright stood smoking by the barrack-room door. S.C.M. Greenaway approached wearing blues, on his way to the sergeants' mess.

He stopped and smiled. Lilburne had been a favourite of his since a bosomy young woman in a sports car had called one afternoon at the guardroom, as she said, to take him for a run. Lilburne knew that this must be one of his father's fantastic plans.

'Who's that?' said Greenaway, staring openly at a pair of well-exposed knees.

'My next leave address, I hope,' whispered Lilburne.

The S.C.M. smiled appreciatively. Ever since, Officer-Cadet Lilburne had been in his eyes a 'character'.

This evening he felt he could relax sufficiently to accept a cigarette. Arkwright lit it for him. The air was still and the warmth of the day lingered.

'All behind you now, you know,' observed the S.C.M.

The two cadets nodded happily.

A crash, a howl, and a flood of obscene language from the hut behind them.

S.C.M. Greenaway jerked the cigarette from his mouth. 'What the hell's that?' he demanded.

'It's Scovington, sir,' said Arkwright. 'We're giving him a good wash before tomorrow. Only cold water, I'm afraid, and a broom. He's a bit reluctant about that sort of thing.'

Greenaway gaped at him for a moment. 'Christ,' he breathed, 'and him a bleeding lord!'

He threw his cigarette to the ground, straightened his tunic, and, moving smartly, marched away.

The arch of his back betrayed his indignation and surprise. 'Cadets,' he said to himself, 'cadets.' He almost forgot to salute an officer, glimpsed briefly a hundred yards away.

July 8th broke warm and sunny. A few dust-particles floated in the clear air. The blue sky, cloudless, canopied the parade-ground.

Three long lines of cadets, their burnished bayonets reflecting the sun, faced the saluting base.

Parents and relations, bowlers and regimental ties alternating with flowered dresses and Ascot hats, sat expectantly in a roped-off enclosure facing the parade, guarded by two cadets with lances.

The band finished a selection from a musical comedy, the drill adjutant's horse fidgeted nervously.

'By God, we've made it!' whispered Lilburne out of the corner of his mouth. Arkwright said nothing but looked towards the enclosure where his mother sat, still in a dark dress, but with a gay hat for the occasion. He wondered what she felt about it all. She looked lonely. The Hussar regiment into which he was to be commissioned was in Malaya. He blinked his eyes as he thought about John, he resolved to write often to his mother. Arkwright marched from his position to stand behind and to the right of Churchouse.

R.S.M. Muxlow signalled with his pace-stick. The drill adjutant drew his sword. He brought the parade to the slope. A shuffling as the band brought their instruments to the ready.

The inspecting officer, Major-General Hakeman, C.B., D.S.O., M.C., stepped on to the saluting base. The drill adjutant threw back his head.

'Parade, General Salute, pre—sent arms.'

The rifles crashed. The spectators rose, bowler hats were removed, and the band burst into the jerky accelerated strains of the salute.

'Good, good,' growled S.C.M. Greenaway encouragingly from the rear.

'Open order . . . march!'

The General began slowly to inspect the line, preceded by two cadets wearing white cross-belts, and followed by the Commandant and an arrow-head of aides and functionaries.

'Centre and rear ranks stand at ease.'

The band began to play a slow waltz for the inspection.

Ransome in the centre rank felt his eyelids pricking. The music, the pageantry. He thought of his father, who during the depression of the twenties had joined the Royal Horse Artillery. Not because he was keen on guns or horses but because the depot was near at Woolwich and because it meant one less mouth to feed in a large family. Ransome had never mentioned this at Ypres. He had thought that among cadets, some of whose fathers had been generals, this might, if known, prejudice his chances. Five years his father had served, becoming a bombardier and fighting in a tribal war on the North-West Frontier. Ransome knew his father was quietly proud of him; he wished he had told somebody at Ypres, though. His thoughts wandered to Lilburne and that girl Jo Mason.

'Rear rank, 'shun, centre rank, stand at ease.' The back of the drill adjutant's neck was becoming red with the effort.

The General looked at the lines of young faces staring woodenly into the middle distance. Reminded him of Sandhurst, that tune the band was playing. 'The Phantom Brigade', it was called. They used to play that. He had been a senior under-officer. Of his junior under-officers one had gained the V.C., the other had bounced cheques.

He stared intently at a tall gunner cadet. Why had his son volunteered for that hare-brained operation in the Western Desert? Only his daughter left, married to that advertising chap. Doubt if they'd have any children. If they did, probably be daughters or queers or pacifists or Socialists.

What had old Risaldar Major Ahmed Khan said when she had been born at Secunderabad? 'A mother of soldiers.'

General Hakeman quickened his pace at the sight of a blue turban. He paused before a bearded Sikh before returning to the saluting base.

'Parade will march past in slow and quick time,' yelled the drill adjutant.

The senior under-officers began to shout at their companies. Churchouse prayed that nothing would go wrong. R.S.M. Muxlow on the flank watched a near-perfect left form. Good voice Churchouse, he thought.

The band crashed out the steady rhythm of the slow march.

'Scipio', thought R.S.M. Muxlow, how many times had he heard that? How many cadets had he trained here and at Sandhurst? Quite a few commanded regiments now. One was a brigadier. They came and saw him and talked about old times. He knew they looked on him as a character. These cadets today—tomorrow he'd have to salute them. He was due to retire in a year or so. Had he been wise to stay in the ranks? George Kemp who had been a corporal at Caterham was now a major. He'd met a lieutenant-colonel the other day who had been in the ranks of the Grenadiers when he had been a company sergeant-major.

He clutched his pace-stick. 'A' Company's dressing was going wrong. Juniors needed more practice before they came on this parade. He'd have to get a grip on C.S.M. Dickens.

General Hakeman braced himself and came to the salute as the first line of faces swivelled simultaneously to meet his gaze. Old Muxlow was a marvel, he thought.

The parade went by again in quick time and then a pause. The cadets stood easy. Churchouse was presented with a silver-embossed cane as the best cadet of the course. He exchanged a word with the General, retired, saluted, and marched back to his post like an automaton.

So long as England produced lads like that, thought the General, we'll be all right.

A microphone was placed in front of the General. He began a short speech.

The loudspeaker was not too clear. 'Young man myself once . . . like you . . . after many years . . . merit recognized . . . qualities of an officer . . . integrity.' Lilburne smiled to himself. A favourite word of his headmaster's. He looked for his parents in the enclosure and found them, surprisingly, together. What was his father up to, sending that girl Elizabeth down here?

'Going out into the world . . . leading the finest soldiers. Short time . . . great privilege . . . worthy of it. Good luck to you all.'

The microphone was removed smartly.

The drill adjutant shifted his weight in the saddle. Not much longer, he thought. What had Diana said, 'Playing at toy soldiers with a lot of schoolboys'? She could be a bitch at times. Now this picture in all the evening papers of his sister dancing on a table in a négligée. Debs were all pretty odd, but this would do him no good in the Brigade, he felt.

If only Diana would marry him.

Muxlow was in place. The passing-out troop was in front of the parade, facing the steps.

'Passing-out troop, inwards turn,' shouted the drill adjutant.

He turned his left hand in the reins. Not really used to the band, this damned horse.

'Passing-out troop, by the centre, slow march.

'Remainder, present arms!'

A crash of rifles and of right heels. The drums rolled, the band burst into 'Auld Lang Syne'. 'G' Squadron advanced rigidly up the steps in threes. The drill adjutant followed them on his horse, as tradition demanded.

The taxi driver switched off his engine. The meter ticked on. Inside, Ransome felt gingerly at his Royal Tank Regiment beret. Churchouse lugged at his Sam Browne. Arkwright stretched his legs in his new trousers.

'What the hell has Charles got up to? We'll miss the train,' he said.

'Here he is,' said Churchouse. He eased the peaked cap of the Life Guards from his nose to get a better view.

A familiar figure struggling with a grip half ran down the road. A young cadet on a bicycle rode past the taxi.

It was well known at Ypres that cadets were not commissioned until midnight and therefore not entitled to salutes from their former comrades or instructors.

Perhaps it was the cherry trousers of the 11th Hussars that Lilburne wore that did the trick. Perhaps he was just a very new cadet.

His head turned smartly to the right. The cycle wobbled. Three paces from Lilburne his right hand snapped up to the salute. The front wheel turned at an alarming angle. Lilburne started, remembered, and acknowledged his first salute carelessly.

Thereby released, the cadet grabbed at a disappearing handlebar with his right hand. He missed. His cycle drove into a hedge, the front wheel lunged into the ditch on the other side as the cadet spread-eagled over the handlebars.

Lilburne threw his bag into the taxi. Churchouse banged the door shut. The taxi accelerated. Lilburne self-consciously hitched at the knees of his cherry trousers.

'Bloody idle, that cadet,' said Ransome.